WORTH THE WAIT

CRYSTAL LAKE SERIES

LAURA SCOTT

READSCAPE PUBLISHING, LLC

WORTH THE WAIT

Book 4 in the Crystal Lake Series

by

Laura Scott

WORTH THE WAIT

CRYSTAL LAKE SERIES (LISTED IN ORDER)

Healing Her Heart

A Soldier's Promise

Coming Home

Worth The Wait

Christmas Reunion

Other Love Inspired Suspense Books

The Thanksgiving Target

Secret Agent Father

The Christmas Rescue

Lawman-In-Charge

Proof Of Life

Identity Crisis*

Twin Peril*

Undercover Cowboy*

Her Mistletoe Protector*

Wrongly Accused (SWAT Series)

Down To The Wire (SWAT Series)

Under The Lawman's Protection (SWAT Series)

Forgotten Memories (SWAT Series)

Holiday On The Run (SWAT Series)

*Stories with Linked Characters

"Dr. Katy?" ER nurse Janelle Larson poked her head through the doorway of the patient's room. "The trauma pager just went off. We have two GSWs on their way in."

Katy Reichert glanced up from the wound she was currently suturing on a young man who'd been sliced by a knife in a bar fight. Now they were getting two gunshot wounds? Barely nine o'clock on a Saturday evening and already patients were pouring in. "Thanks, Janelle. I'll be finished here shortly."

"Sounds good. I'll make sure the trauma bays are well stocked." Janelle flashed a quick smile and darted back out of the room.

Katy concentrated on finishing her task, even as her stomach clenched with anxiety. Hope County Hospital wasn't normally so busy, but with spring giving way to summer, it seemed that locals and tourists alike were determined to celebrate the warm weather by drinking too much and getting into fights. She couldn't remember the last time they'd had so many patients, especially at the same time.

Although, truthfully, she'd had far worse nights when she'd been practicing at Baltimore General.

She shied away from the painful memories of her past and focused on the issue at hand. Her patient, Danny Truitt, snored loudly, no doubt from the combination of the alcohol he'd consumed prior to the knife fight and the pain medication he'd been given here. She finished up Danny's sutures—fourteen in all—stripped off her gloves, washed her hands, then quickly logged in to the computer to complete her orders.

"All finished?" Merry Crain, another ER nurse, asked as she breezed into the room.

"Yes, but we'll need to monitor him closely until he sobers up. We can't discharge him until he's fully awake."

"I'll get him hooked up to the telemetry and pulse ox," Merry agreed. "That way we'll hear the alarms if his condition changes."

"Good idea. We'll need all hands on deck for the traumas." Katy headed over toward the trauma bay, anxious to hear more about their impending arrivals. She looked around but didn't see her colleague, trauma surgeon Wade Matthews. Where was he? He was the trauma surgeon on call; his pager should have gone off by now, alerting him to the GSWs.

Janelle was standing near the computer, making sure everything was ready to go. Katy stripped off her lab coat and tossed it over one of the chairs along the back counter that housed several computers before crossing over to Janelle.

"What do we know so far?" she asked.

"Not much. One patient has a gunshot wound to the upper chest, and the other has a gunshot wound to the arm," Janelle said. "They should be here any minute."

Katy nodded. "We should put University Hospital in Madison on alert for the GSW to the chest."

"I already made the call," Janelle assured her. "It's protocol to let them know about serious traumas. The Lifeline helicopter is on its way. They've agreed to remain on standby up on the landing pad."

Katy nodded, wishing they'd dispatched the chopper to the scene. But it was too late now. She took a deep breath and let it out slowly. Seconds later, the double doors leading in from the ambulance bay burst open, and a bevy of people crowded through.

"GSW to the chest, bleeding badly," the paramedic announced. "We've been pumping O neg blood into him like crazy."

Since there was still no sign of Wade Matthews, Katy had no choice but to step up and take control. "Get the level one rapid infuser," she ordered. "Give four units of O neg, and order some fresh frozen plasma as well. I need a set of vitals as soon as possible."

Janelle deftly connected the tubing and began hanging blood products. Another nurse began connecting the patient to the heart monitor.

"Merry, find Dr. Matthews, *stat!*" Katy drew on gloves and a gown over her scrubs, anticipating blood splatters. She lifted the dressing from the patient's upper-left chest. Blood pooled rapidly, indicating a nicked artery and, likely, a severely injured lobe of the lung. She wasn't a surgeon, but if she didn't take immediate action, this man would bleed to death.

"Get me a chest tray and suction," she ordered. "And start a propofol drip to put him under. I need to explore this wound."

Janelle shoved the chest tray on a bedside table located

to her right, and Katy forced herself to remain calm as she waited for the nurse to begin the propofol infusion so that her patient wouldn't feel any pain. She sent up a silent prayer for strength as she picked up the scalpel. A bead of sweat trickled down the side of her face when she opened the entry wound so that she could assess the damage.

Somehow, she managed to drown out the cacophony of voices surrounding her to focus on the emergency situation at hand. She needed to find a way to stop the bleeding. Through the opening, she could see the bullet was lodged in the upper lobe of the lung, which wasn't good. But when she continued her search and found a lacerated artery, pumping out blood at an alarming rate, her stomach dropped.

She hadn't repaired an artery this large or removed a significant portion of lung tissue since her residency, but what choice did she have? How else could she stop the bleeding and remove the bullet? Performing surgery wasn't her strong suit, but she knew they needed to buy time in order to stabilize the patient so he could be flown to Madison.

"Hand me a scalpel," she forced herself to say, hoping the tremor in her tone didn't betray her lack of confidence. The only positive note was that the injury was located high enough that she didn't need to split the patient's chest.

With the scalpel in hand, she opened the entrance wound and placed small vascular clamps to stop the bleeding. She'd need to work fast, or the surrounding tissue would die from lack of oxygen. She sutured the artery, silently praying for strength and precision. When the artery was repaired to the best of her ability, she opened the clamps and breathed a sigh of relief when the bleeding was contained.

Feeling calmer now that the most tenuous part was

done, she picked up the forceps and began exploring the upper lobe of the lung where the bullet was lodged. She found herself glancing frequently at the overhead monitor, to make sure her patient remained stable. Halfway through the procedure, Wade Matthews finally showed up.

"You're doing fine," he said, as if his absence was no big deal. She glared at him, seriously annoyed, but this wasn't the time or place to vent her frustration. "I'll take it from here," he assured her.

She stepped back, knowing Wade's surgical skills were far better than hers, although he wasn't a cardiothoracic surgeon either. "The chopper is ready to take him to Madison, so the goal is to stabilize him enough for the flight."

Wade nodded but didn't look up from the wound. A glance up at the heart monitor convinced her that their patient was doing all right, not great, but better than she'd expected. Her gaze dropped to the patient's face, and her stomach squeezed painfully when she realized the guy was far younger than she'd originally thought—which might be why he was still alive, despite the serious injuries to his artery and lung.

For a moment, Steffie's all-too-still features flashed in her mind, reminding her of the young patient she'd failed back in Baltimore.

"Dr. Katy? Should we get more blood?" Janelle asked, breaking into her thoughts.

"Yes, keep the O neg flowing," she said. She stripped off her gloves and turned to look for the second GSW patient. Her gaze landed on DNR game warden Reese Webster sitting on a gurney with a field dressing wrapped around his left bicep. She'd taken care of Reese just a few weeks earlier, after he'd been slashed by a wounded bear, so she shouldn't be surprised to see him again. Apparently his job often put him in the path of danger.

As she walked toward him, he didn't glance at her, his gaze focused solely on the patient with the chest wound. He seemed more concerned about the other guy than his own injury.

Katy put a hand on Reese's forearm, the warmth of his skin practically scorching her fingers. She dropped her hand, hoping he didn't notice her hasty retreat. "You should probably lie down so I can take a look at your arm."

Reese's mouth tightened, and he shook his head. "Sorry, Dr. Katy, but I'm fine. Marcus Boyle is the one who needs your medical attention, not me."

She looked over her shoulder to see that Wade had finished with the procedure and was placing fresh dressings over the open chest wound.

"Get those units of blood in, stat, so we can get him up to the helipad," he ordered. "Now!"

Hospital staff and paramedics jumped to do his bidding. Janelle pushed the rapid infuser with the blood transfusions going alongside the gurney, while the other staff members quickly wheeled the patient to the elevators leading up to the roof, where the helipad was located. As soon as they left the trauma bay, an eerie silence filled the room.

"Which hospital are they taking him to?" Reese asked.

"University Hospital in Madison," she replied. "Trust me, he has the best chance of surviving his injury there. They have highly qualified cardiothoracic surgeons on staff. What we did here was a temporary patch job."

Reese stared at the closed elevator door for a long moment. "It's my fault he's injured," he said in a low voice.

"I'm sure there's more to that story," she murmured, feeling bad for him. "Now let me take a look at your arm."

Reese sighed and finally stretched out on the gurney. He was still wearing his forest-green uniform, and he was so tall his booted feet dangled off the end of the cart.

"I shot him," he said bluntly.

Katy unwrapped the bloody gauze from Reese's arm, wincing in sympathy when she saw fresh blood oozing down his arm. His uniform sleeve had been hacked off super short, no doubt by the paramedics to provide easy access to the wound. "I'm thinking he shot you first," she said. "You're lucky the bullet went all the way through. This looks to be mostly a flesh wound."

Reese didn't argue or flinch as she probed the wound, making sure there were no foreign bodies left behind. But when she noted a few threads of fabric embedded inside, she grew concerned.

"I need to irrigate this with antibiotic solution, okay? I can't remember from last time you were here if you have any allergies?"

"No allergies," he said tersely.

All three nurses had gone up with the chest wound patient to the helipad, so she stripped off her gloves to get the normal saline, antibiotic solution, and syringes that she needed.

"Why did he shoot you?" she asked as a way to distract herself from the odd awareness she experienced from being so close to him. She'd come to Crystal Lake, Wisconsin, to get away from the memories of her past failures, not to be distracted by a handsome game warden.

"He was poaching and has been for a long time. I'm sure he injured that bear that clawed me three weeks ago. I've been tracking him ever since, and this time, I caught him in the act of shooting a cougar." Reese's tone was hard and flat. "When I confronted him, he fired at me, so I shot back."

"A cougar?" she echoed in horror. While she loved working in the Hope County Hospital ER, she was a city girl at heart. All this talk of bears and cougars living in the woods that flanked the north side of the lake unnerved her. She enjoyed hiking the walking/running path but wouldn't dare venture any farther. "You're joking, right? There really aren't cougars around here."

A wry grin tugged at his mouth, making him even more handsome. As if his dark hair, hazel-green eyes and broad shoulders weren't devastating enough? "Just a few, and don't worry, they tend to stay far away from people. They're feeding on the overpopulation of deer, which is a good thing."

Feeding on Bambi was a good thing? Katy suppressed a shiver. "If you say so," she muttered doubtfully. "Do you want some pain medication?" she asked, changing the subject. "This is going to hurt."

"No pain meds," Reese said firmly. "I need to drive up to Madison to check on how Boyle is doing."

She wanted to roll her eyes at his macho attitude, but she remembered how Reese had declined pain meds the last time he was here too. With a mental shrug, she went to work, extensively irrigating the wound and then turning toward her suture tray.

"Are you sure you don't want something for pain before I stitch this up?" she asked, stalling for time. Maybe if she waited long enough, Wade would return, and he could do the task. After all, he owed her big-time. Not that Reese's wound needed a trauma surgeon, but for some reason, she loathed the idea of sticking needles into Reese.

"I'm sure."

She stared at him for a long minute before taking a deep breath and picking up the curved needle attached to a suture. Once again, she sent up a silent prayer, knowing she needed extra support from her faith. When she pierced the needle through the edge of his wound, she flinched more than he did. She tried to think of Reese like any other patient, but it wasn't easy. Sweat dampened her scalp and rolled down her back as she placed one suture after another, closing the entry wound and then the exit wound.

And when she finally finished, she stepped back and dropped the suture needle on a wave of relief. For a moment, her vision went hazy, and Reese unexpectedly reached out and clasped her arm in a strong, firm grip.

"Are you all right?" he asked with concern.

She forced a smile. "Of course. You're the patient here, not me."

He lifted an eyebrow, and she inwardly sighed, knowing she wasn't fooling him one bit. She stared down at his hand holding her arm, and he slowly released her.

She forced a smile. "Sorry, I guess I'm a little tired. It's been a busy night."

His expression turned serious. "I know. You were really incredible."

She blushed and dropped her gaze, knowing that if he knew the truth about what had happened in Baltimore, he wouldn't think of her as incredible at all. Her heart squeezed in her chest, and she pulled herself together with an effort.

"Okay, you're all set to go, but I want you to take antibiotics twice daily for the next ten days," she said in a stern tone. "And you'll need to make an appointment with your doctor to get the sutures removed."

"I don't have a doctor," he said with a frown. "Can't I just come back here to see you?"

For a moment, she simply looked at him, wondering if she was imagining the flash of interest in his gaze.

Of course she was. She barely knew the man, had only patched him up twice now. What was wrong with her? She wasn't interested in anything remotely resembling a relationship. She needed to get a grip and fast.

"I'm an ER doctor; I don't have clinic appointments," she managed. "But you can establish care with any of the general medicine physicians here. In fact, I'll be happy to give you a list of names."

He shrugged. "No need, I'll just come back when you're working," he said in a casual tone. He nimbly jumped off the gurney, looming over her from his height of six feet three inches. She craned her neck, tilting her face upward, thinking it was ridiculous that the top of her head barely reached his chin.

"I appreciate everything you've done for me," he said in a low tone. "Thank you."

Their gazes crashed and held. For the life of her, she couldn't manage a single coherent thought. Thankfully, the rest of the medical team returned from the helipad. The moment was gone, and she stepped back gratefully. Wade Matthews disappeared down the hallway while Janelle began cleaning up the equipment and restocking supplies in the first trauma bay.

"Dr. Katy?" Merry called, entering the room with a worried frown etched in her forehead. "I heard the heart monitor beeping and found Danny thrashing around in his room. I think his pain meds have worn off, even though he still reeks of alcohol."

"Okay, don't give him any more pain meds yet. I'll be right over," she promised, grateful for the interruption. She crossed over to the counter, drew her lab coat back on and then rummaged for a prescription pad. Her fingers shook a bit as she filled out the antibiotic order for Reese. When she finished, she carried it over to him. "Here, you can get this filled at any pharmacy, and you need to take these until they're gone. I'd recommend taking your first dose tonight."

"Thanks," he said, taking the script and tucking it in his pocket. "See you soon, Katy."

"Sure," she murmured, distracted by his use of her given name. It took a herculean effort on her part to turn away to head toward Danny's room.

Maybe it was her imagination working overtime, but she could swear she felt Reese's gaze boring into her back as she walked away.

2

Reese walked outside, leaving Dr. Katy and the rest of the ER staff behind. It wasn't until he was standing in front of the ER parking lot searching through the darkness for his car that he realized he didn't have his truck here because he'd been brought in by the ambulance crew.

Idiot. That's what happened when he let his hormones run wild.

He shook his head in disgust. Hadn't he already learned the hard way that relationships weren't worth the trouble? His ex-wife had left him for his best friend after cleaning out every last dime in their joint bank account. Three years later, he was still digging his way out of debt.

The last thing he needed was to start down that path again, especially not with a pretty redheaded doctor who likely made more than twice his salary, and then some.

With a rueful grimace, he focused on the present and pulled out his phone. He could try one of his DNR buddies even though it was almost ten thirty. He grimaced, hating to bother them on a Saturday night. But considering there wasn't any sort of taxi service in Crystal Lake, he didn't have much choice.

Gavin's phone went straight to voice mail. Doug's phone rang a half dozen times before going to voice mail. He tried George's number, too, with no luck.

Where was everyone? Obviously they all had better things to do on a Saturday night than he did. Which was why he'd been working, following Boyle's trail through the woods. If only he'd gotten there sooner, before the idiot had killed the cougar.

He scowled at his phone. So now what? The only option he could think of was to call the Hope County Sheriff's Department to request a ride. The DNR worked closely with local law enforcement agencies—surely someone would be willing to help him out.

As if on cue, a sheriff's department vehicle pulled into the ER parking lot. Reese waited for the deputy to climb out from behind the wheel before walking toward him.

"Hi, Deputy Armbruster, right? I don't know if you remember me, but my name is Reese Webster, and I work for the DNR," he said.

"Yes, I remember and you're just the guy I'm looking for," the deputy said dryly. "I need to take your statement."

Great, he thought with a sigh. "All right, but afterwards, will you give me a lift back to my truck? The ambulance brought me in, and I need a ride."

"I suppose." The deputy didn't sound too thrilled. "Let's go inside. I need to know how the alleged poacher is doing."

Reese wrestled with his temper as he fell into step beside the deputy, whose name tag identified his last name as Armbruster. "The poacher's name is Marcus Boyle, and he's on his way to Madison for treatment. He's a confirmed poacher. I personally watched him shoot that cougar, and when I yelled out to stop him, he shot me. Feel free to add attempted murder to his arrest warrant."

Armbruster glanced at the bandage on his upper arm. "Right now, it's your word against his, isn't it?"

"Since I work for the state, that makes me the more credible witness," he responded sharply. Was this guy for real? "And when I find the body of the cougar he killed, you'll be able to match the ballistics of his gun to the slug in the cat."

"Okay, okay," Deputy Armbruster said, holding up his hand in defense. They entered the ER and crossed over to the waiting area. "I believe you, but that doesn't mean I don't need to tie up all the loose ends."

There weren't any loose ends, but he forced himself to bite back the sarcasm. "Listen, I've been tracking this guy for the last month. I have photos of his boot prints along with the slug we took out of the bear he shot. I've built an iron-clad case around this guy, and I'm happy to share everything I have to put him behind bars."

"Once he's out of the hospital, right?" Deputy Armbruster pointed out wryly.

"Yeah, once he's out of the hospital," he echoed. Reese didn't like knowing Boyle could easily die of his gunshot wound, a wound that he was responsible for. He much preferred that the guy recover so he could pay for his crimes.

"What happened after you shot him?" Armbruster asked.

"I called for help and hauled him on a tarp out to the clearing." Reese remembered wishing for help from Duke, his German shepherd, as he struggled to drag Boyle's dead weight. Luckily, the ambulance crew had met him halfway or Boyle might not have made it.

Still might not make it.

"Hmm," Armbruster murmured as he scribbled in his tattered notebook. "I'm sorry, but we have to confiscate your gun, to validate the ballistics report."

Reese ground his teeth together but handed over his weapon. He knew the protocol, and his boss, Gavin Crowley, would have taken it if the deputy hadn't asked for it.

"Thanks. Anything else?"

Reese hesitated, wondering if he should voice all his suspicions. He didn't have any concrete proof that Boyle hadn't been working alone, just a few glimpses of a blond dude in the same area where Boyle tended to illegally hunt. The blond dude was good, though; Reese hadn't even found a boot print or any other evidence that he'd been working with Boyle.

"Nothing else from the incident this evening," he confirmed. He'd glimpsed the blond dude about an hour before Boyle had shot the cougar, so either he'd stayed hidden once Reese had shouted at Boyle, or seeing the guy had been some strange coincidence.

"Okay, thanks." Armbruster flipped his notebook shut.

"So about that ride," he began, but the deputy's radio squawked, and Armbruster turned away to listen.

"Ten-four," he said. "Sorry, Webster, but there's a crash on the highway, and I'm the closest deputy. Gotta run. If you're still here later, try me again." Armbruster rose to his feet and headed back outside.

Reese watched the deputy leave with a sigh. He pulled out his phone again, knowing that if none of his buddies answered their phones, he might be stuck here for hours.

He'd finished leaving another round of voice mail messages and was trying to think of another alternative for a ride when he caught sight of Katy walking toward him, a frown puckering her brow. He abruptly disconnected from the call and rose to his feet.

"What's wrong?" she asked. "Is your arm hurting? Or did you have a reaction to the antibiotics?"

"No, I haven't even picked up the antibiotics yet." He flashed a lopsided smile, hating the thought of asking her for a favor. "I'm waiting for a ride," he added lamely.

Her frown cleared, and she glanced out toward the parking lot. Did he imagine the hesitation in her tone? "My shift is over and I'm leaving now. I'm happy to give you a ride."

"Are you sure?" Her offer was exactly what he needed, but for some reason he felt guilty for taking her up on it. Not that he'd planned to get shot and stranded here. He should have insisted on driving himself.

"Of course I'm sure." Any hesitation she might have had seemed to have evaporated. "We'll stop at the pharmacy first," she added. "I wasn't kidding about those antibiotics."

"I really appreciate your help," he said, quickening his pace so he could hold the door open for her. "Deputy Armbruster was called out to the scene of a crash, so I might have had to wait for hours."

"It's really no problem," she assured him.

Reese followed Katy through the darkness as she headed for her car. His fingers itched to take her keys so he could drive, but he sensed she wouldn't appreciate it. She pressed the key fob, and the lights flashed on. He opened her driver's-side door and closed it behind her, before rounded the vehicle to slide in the passenger seat.

She turned on the engine and pulled out of the parking space. "Any particular pharmacy?" she asked.

"There's one on Main Street, right?" he said, thinking

back to when he'd had to get antibiotics after the bear incident. "I should be on record there."

"Sounds good," she said, turning left toward Main Street, which was all downtown Crystal Lake had to offer.

Reese sat back, trying to think of something to say. He was so out of practice being with a woman it wasn't funny. "I hope I'm not taking you too far out of your way," he said. "My truck is way over on the north side of the lake."

"As long as you protect me from cougars and bears, I'll be fine." Her light teasing tone helped him relax.

"No problem," he agreed. His stomach growled loudly, and he pressed his hand to his abdomen, trying to make it shut up.

"Look, Rose's Café is still open. Why don't we stop for a bite to eat?" she suggested.

He wasn't fooled by her innocent tone, but since the idea of having one of the best burgers in town was too good to pass up, he decided to let it go. "That's a great idea. My treat since you're going out of your way to drive me to my truck."

For a moment, he feared she'd insist on paying, making him a bigger bum than he already felt, but then she nodded, offering a small smile. "All right, it's a deal."

She parked in front of the drug store, which wasn't too far from Rose's Café. She waited for him inside the pharmacy and, thankfully, filling the script didn't take long. He paid for the medication and then tucked the bottle into the front pocket of his uniform slacks.

"All set?" she asked as he returned.

"Yes, Doctor," he teased.

She rolled her eyes. "You'd be surprised how many of our patients are not compliant with their medications."

"I can imagine," he said, wondering if she was reminding him of their patient/doctor relationship on purpose. Not that he really blamed her, since this wasn't anything close to a date.

She fell silent as they walked down the crowded sidewalk toward Rose's. Again, he searched for a safe topic of conversation but realized he didn't know very much about her, other than she was an amazing doctor.

His stomach rumbled again, reminding him that he hadn't eaten since lunch. He opened the door of the café, relieved to notice there were several empty booths.

"Hi, Dr. Katy, and Reese, it's been a long time," Josie greeted them from behind the counter, her eyes bright with curiosity. Josie was one of the biggest gossips in town, and he inwardly groaned at the way she kept glancing between them. "Have a seat. I'll be right over."

Katy slid into the first available booth, and he took the seat across from her. "She'll have us married by morning," he whispered with a wink.

Katy's cheeks turned pink, and she suppressed a laugh. "She's been trying to set me up since I got here," she whispered back. "Maybe now she'll back off."

Reese chuckled. "I'll take the heat for you, no problem."

Josie bustled over, plopping two plastic menus in front of them. "So what can I get you?" she asked. It took her a moment to notice the bandage covering his arm. "Reese, what on earth happened?"

"Just a scratch," he said, waving off her concern. "Nothing to worry about. I'd like a large glass of water, please, and one of your amazing burgers loaded with the works."

Josie preened at his praise. "One burger with the works coming up. What about you, Dr. Katy?"

"Chicken sandwich, and I'll have water, too, please."

"Great. So, I see you're still wearing your scrubs; you

must have come straight from the hospital, huh?" Josie said, clearly prying for more information.

Katy's smile was strained. "Yes, and it was so busy I didn't get dinner. I'm famished."

"Oh, you poor thing." Josie looked appalled at the idea of missing a meal. "I'll get your food going right away. Now you two just sit back and relax for a bit, okay?"

"We will, thanks," Katy said.

Reese shook his head as Josie headed back toward the kitchen. "Talk about being nosy. Nice ploy to get sympathy, though. At least she'll hurry up with our food."

"No kidding," she murmured. She sat back in her seat with a sigh. "But it wasn't exactly a ploy. I really was too busy to eat."

He felt bad, knowing that he'd played a role in her missing dinner. "I'm not sure how you manage to keep so cool under pressure," he said.

The smile faded from her face, and her cheeks went pale moments before she ducked her head, making him realize he'd hit a nerve. "It's nothing."

It was far from nothing, but obviously she didn't want to talk about it. "I hope Boyle is hanging in there. I'd feel terrible if he died after all your hard work."

"I'm sure he'll be fine." She cleared her throat awkwardly. "Tell me how you managed to stumble across him at the exact moment she shot a cougar."

Accepting her change of topic, he explained how he'd been tracking the guy for weeks, gathering the evidence he needed. Josie came out with their food as he finished telling her about his conversation with Deputy Armbruster.

"Here you go," Josie said cheerfully.

"Looks great," he said with a broad smile. "Thanks."

"No problem." Josie walked away and began wiping

down a perfectly clean table well within earshot of their booth.

Katy didn't seem to notice, bowing her head and closing her eyes. Reese was surprised to realize she was praying. Despite the fact that he hadn't been to church since Suzanne had left, he bowed his head, too, respectfully waiting for her to finish.

"Looks fabulous," she said, meeting his gaze without a hint of embarrassment.

"Yeah," he agreed, although he wasn't talking about the food. Katy's deep red hair was pulled back in a fancy braid, but little wisps had fallen down around her face, making her look softer, more feminine. He forced himself to pry his gaze away and to concentrate on his meal.

For the next few minutes, they were both too busy eating to say much, and Josie finally left them alone, returning to her perch behind the counter.

Katy finished before he did, and he gestured to what was left of his burger. "Do you want to try a bite?" he asked.

She laughed and shook her head. "No, thanks, although I'm glad you're enjoying it. Don't forget to take your antibiotic."

"I won't." To prove his point, he drew out the bottle and took one of the pills. His arm still throbbed painfully, but he ignored it, finishing the last few bites of his meal. Josie returned with their check, so he tucked the antibiotics away and pulled out his wallet.

"How was everything?" Josie asked.

"Wonderful," Katy said with a smile.

"Ditto," he quipped, glancing at the bill. He pulled out more than enough cash, leaving a nice tip. "We need to get going, but thanks again, Josie."

"You're welcome," Josie said, tucking the generous tip in her pocket. "You two come back soon, you hear?"

Katy blushed again, and he swallowed a laugh, steering her toward the door.

"With any luck, the gossip will die down in a few days," Katy said with an apologetic smile. "I hope your, uh, family will understand."

Amused, he glanced down at her. "No family, no girl-friend, no one to care about any gossip," he said. "What about you? Is someone close to you going to be upset?"

"No, I'm not really close to my family. No siblings and after my parents split up, they created their own lives with their respective spouses," she said as they approached her car. "I don't hear much from the friends I left behind in Baltimore."

So that's where the slight Eastern accent in her tone came from. The fact that they were both alone here in Crystal Lake ironically made him feel closer to her. Which was stupid, considering they were complete opposites.

"Which way to your truck?" she asked, cranking her key in the ignition.

He gave her directions, hoping she'd be able to make it home okay after she dropped him off.

"Are you sure this is the road?" she asked, frowning as she peered through the windshield.

"I'm sure. My truck should be right around the next curve."

She slowed her small car, taking the curve carefully as if she were afraid she'd miss it. But sure enough, his truck was right where he'd left it.

As they came closer, he frowned, realizing he'd been wrong. His truck wasn't at all the way he'd left it.

Someone had smashed every window, leaving shards of

glass everywhere. The sides were dented in and each of the four tires had been slashed. The vehicle was so badly damaged he couldn't imagine there was any way to repair it.

"What happened?" Katy asked in a horrified whisper.

He let out a heavy breath, raking his gaze around the wooded area. He hoped that whoever had destroyed his truck was long gone, but couldn't afford to take that chance.

"Don't stop," he said sharply. "Speed up and keep going. I'll call the sheriff's department. Unfortunately, it looks as if I'll need a ride home."

"Someone is really mad at you," she said in a shaky voice, punching the accelerator with enough force to pin him to his seat. "That was no accident."

No, it wasn't. And his gut churned with anger as he realized the blond dude he'd seen lurking in the woods near Boyle was likely responsible.

Too bad he had no idea who the guy was or where to find him.

3

Katy struggled to relax her white-knuckled grip on the steering wheel. Every nerve in her body was stretched to the breaking point. The violence that had been taken out on Reese's truck had shaken her to the core.

She was used to caring for victims of crimes in the trauma room, but knowing that someone had it out for Reese on a personal level made her feel sick to her stomach.

Listening to his one-sided conversation with the sheriff's deputy wasn't making her feel any better.

"Take a right at the next intersection," he said after disconnecting from the call.

She slowed her car for the turn, wishing the wooded highway had bright streetlights like those she was used to seeing in the city. But out here in the middle of nowhere, she only had her headlights to cut through the absolute blackness of the night.

"My driveway is about halfway down the road. See the little red fire signs? I'm number 872."

"Red fire signs?" She stepped on the brake and peered

through the windshield. "You mean those tiny, narrow red and white markers?"

"Yep, that's exactly what I mean." He was peering through his passenger-side window, and she was very much afraid he was looking for a glimpse of the person who'd demolished his truck.

"Is this your driveway?" she asked, frowning when she saw the barely there dirt road right after the 872 sign.

"Just drop me off here," Reese instructed. "No need to drive up to the cabin."

"I don't think you should stay here," she said, slowing to a stop. "What if whoever trashed your truck figures out where you live?"

"I have my dog, Duke, to help keep me safe," he assured her. "Do you think you can find your way back home?"

"Of course." She brushed away his concern. "But please don't stay here. I'd be happy to take you and your dog to the motel in town."

Reese hesitated but then reluctantly nodded. "Okay, I'll take you up on your offer. Besides, staying in town will make it easier to rent a car in the morning."

She shifted the car into reverse to back up a few feet, and pulled into the rutted driveway, wincing as she bounced around in her seat. No wonder he owned a truck.

The driveway seemed to stretch on forever—a good hundred yards, by her estimation—before she could make out a cozy log cabin nestled in a small clearing. As they approached, she heard the sound of a dog barking. A big dog, judging by the deep tone of it.

She stopped her car at the edge of the clearing, and Reese popped out of the car. "Duke, quiet," he yelled.

Instantly, the dog fell silent, and even though she didn't know squat about pets, she was impressed.

"I'll be right back," Reese promised. "If you see anything out of the ordinary, lean on the horn."

He disappeared inside the log cabin, leaving her to wonder just what he meant by *out of the ordinary.* Since he was at home with cougars and bears, she figured his definition was far different than hers.

No reason to be afraid; she was surrounded by steel. Surely a bear wasn't strong enough to tip over a car. Or was it? The image that flashed in her mind wasn't reassuring.

Stop it! You're only making yourself crazy.

Katy took a deep breath and let go of the steering wheel, trying to relax. She repeated the action several times, pretending she was in her yoga class, willing the tension to leave her muscles.

Her hard-won sense of peace was shattered when the back passenger-side door to her four-door sedan opened and a mammoth dog jumped in, stuffing his wet nose against the vulnerable area along the side of her neck.

"Ack!" she cried, shrinking away from what looked like a moose masquerading as a dog.

"Down, Duke," Reese commanded. Once again, the dog dropped instantly, stretching out along the backseat as if he owned it. Reese set a box, a laptop case and a duffel bag on the floor before shutting the door.

Before she realized what was happening, Reese was tapping on her driver's-side window. Flustered, she pushed the button to lower it. "What are you doing?" Surely he wasn't going to leave her alone with his massive dog?

"Why don't you let me drive?" he suggested. "The driveway isn't easy to back down, and there are a few stumps in the clearing that might damage the undercarriage of your car."

She swallowed hard and nodded. Keeping a wary eye on

Duke lying across the backseat, she awkwardly crawled over the console and plopped in the passenger side. Reese slid her seat back before climbing in.

"Sorry if Duke scared you," he said, expertly backing down the winding driveway. He went slowly, but even so, the car bounced and jiggled as they went over the ruts. "There's no reason to be afraid. He won't hurt you."

"I...um, never had a pet," she confessed. "And he's really big. Are you sure he's not a wolf?" Seemed only natural to add wolves to the bears and cougars roaming around the woods.

"I'm sure." Reese's white teeth flashed in a quick smile. "Duke is a German shepherd, the breed most often used as police dogs. He's well trained, and I promise he won't hurt you."

"Okay. Good. That's good." She gripped the handrest as he turned onto the highway. It wasn't until they approached Main Street that she realized the Crystal Lake Motel might not allow pets, especially one as large as Duke.

The cute two-bedroom house she'd purchased was located just outside of town, on a small parcel of land with lakefront access. Perfect for a single woman living alone, but not nearly big enough for Reese and his huge dog.

Should she offer to stay at the motel so that Reese could use her house? She shouldn't have to leave her home, but truthfully, she'd rather stay in the motel than be confined in a small space with Duke.

Reese pulled in front of the motel. "Thanks for all your help," he said, handing her the keys. "Give me a minute to grab my things."

"Are you sure the motel will allow you to bring Duke?" she asked, dreading his response.

"Yeah, I've stayed here three years ago when I first took the DNR job. It won't be a problem."

She took the keys with a sense of overwhelming relief. "Okay, then. Let me know if you need anything."

"Sure thing." He opened the door, and she was surprised Duke didn't move until Reese gave him the signal. "Come, Duke."

Duke wagged his tail and leaped out of the car, staying close to Reese's side. Again, she had to admit she was impressed, even though the huge animal had scared her spitless.

Reese left with a wave, striding toward the motel with his duffel and computer case slung over his shoulder and some sort of box tucked beneath his arm. Was that the evidence he'd talked about? Or supplies for the dog?

Didn't matter, she told herself. It was well past midnight, and she was exhausted. Right now, she just wanted to go home.

But even in her familiar surroundings, sleep eluded her. She tried to blame her bout of insomnia on the adrenaline rush from dealing with the gunshot victims and then finding the badly damaged truck, but she knew those weren't the real cause.

Her mind kept returning to Reese. Anyone with half a brain would stay far away from him, considering that he'd been shot recently and had his truck smashed to smithereens. He was the kind of guy who lived in a log cabin and protected the wilderness as a DNR game warden. They were complete and total opposites.

So why couldn't she forget about him?

THE NEXT MORNING, sunlight streamed through her

window, waking her from a restless night far too early. She moaned and pulled her pillow over her head, but it was no use.

With a disgusted sigh, she crawled out of bed, grateful she had the next two days off work. She called the chief medical officer to report Wade Matthews, and then called University Hospital in Madison to check on Marcus Boyle.

She was relieved to hear that Boyle was listed in critical yet stable condition. About fifteen minutes later, her boss returned her call about Wade, promising to talk to him. Satisfied, she filled a cup of coffee and took a seat at her small kitchen table, where she could gaze out over the lake. The events from last night seemed surreal in the bright light of the morning.

It took a minute for her to remember that today was Sunday and that she was scheduled to be a greeter for the midmorning church service.

She finished her coffee and got ready for church. She was early, and as she drove past the motel she pressed on the brake, wondering if she should stop by to see how Reese and Duke were doing.

Wait a minute, what was she thinking? They were fine. Reese was more than capable of taking care of himself, and Duke too. She didn't even like dogs, although that might partially be because she'd never spent any time with them. Regardless, pets were not welcome in church.

Giving herself a mental shake, she sped up and approached the tall white-steeple church. As always, the minute she stepped inside God's house, she felt better. Calmer.

At peace.

She greeted the parishioners as they arrived, recognizing many of her former patients, from the occasional bout of the flu to more serious medical concerns such as having a stroke or heart attack.

On days like today, she was glad she'd made the decision to leave Baltimore. And not just because of Steffie, the young patient she'd lost. The ER at Baltimore General was seriously understaffed. The number of patients she'd treated in an average shift was more than double what she cared for in an entire weekend here at Hope County Hospital. And so far, she hadn't made any mistakes or errors in judgment.

Not yet.

She pushed the sliver of doubt away, determined to keep the nightmares from her past buried deep. The last thing the citizens of Crystal Lake and Hope County needed was for their ER doctor to have doubts about her level of competency.

Katy sat alone toward the back of the church when the service began. She enjoyed Pastor John's approach. He had a way of preaching that was interesting and engaging, without the fire-and-brimstone attitude that she'd sometimes heard before. The theme of his sermon today was keeping the Lord in the forefront of their minds and not just when they needed his strength and support. Katy knew she was guilty of doing exactly that and made a silent promise to do better from here on out.

When the service was over, she scooted out the back, avoiding the usual chatter that many of the parishioners enjoyed. She always felt a bit awkward in social situations like this, mostly because she knew most of the people here from the hospital, which some folks didn't appreciate being reminded about.

"Hi, Dr. Katy," Merry greeted her. "You remember my husband, Zack."

"Of course. How are you both doing?" she asked, smiling at the young couple. Merry had gone through a rough patch last fall, but things seemed to have settled down for her and Zack. In fact, she knew they were in the process of building their dream house on the other side of the lake.

"We're good, but you still look tired. We had a long shift last night, huh?" Merry said with a wry smile.

"Yes, but I called Madison this morning, and you'll be glad to know that our patient is stable."

"Good to hear," Merry said, giving her husband's hand a squeeze. "Zack was all worried about the gunshot wounds we had, but I assured him there was absolutely no danger."

"There was plenty of danger," Zack corrected. "You just got lucky."

An image of Reese's smashed truck floated in her mind, making her tend to agree with him. But she forced a smile. "I imagine Zack is always going to worry about you," she said, sidestepping the comment. "After all, you were hurt on the job once."

"That was different." Merry waved away the incident as inconsequential.

"Well, take care, both of you," Katy said, unwilling to be drawn into their good-natured spat. Although watching the way Zack looked at Merry, pure love shining from his blue eyes, made her heart squeeze in her chest, wishing for something she'd never have.

"You too, Dr. Katy." Merry waved as she and Zack headed toward their car.

She shook off the flash of envy. That was not in keeping with the spirit of Pastor John's sermon. She walked to her car, not in the mood to go back to her empty house.

Yet she wasn't going to stop at the motel, either. Besides, she doubted that Reese and his giant dog were still there.

He'd planned on renting a car, and even though it was Sunday, Hank, the guy who ran Billy's Auto Shop, was always willing to open up for a sure sale.

But what if Billy didn't have a car for sale or for rent? Katy found herself turning left at the stoplight so she could drive past Billy's Auto Shop.

When she saw Reese and Duke walking along the side of the road, she slowed down and lowered her window. "What happened? Didn't Hank have a car for you?"

"Hi, Katy," Reese greeted her. He stepped closer, and Duke followed, staying right by Reese's side. The dog was almost totally black in color and, if possible, looked more menacing in daylight than he had last night. "No, he doesn't have one yet but might by tomorrow."

"Do you need a ride?" she asked.

Reese hesitated, then shook his head. "I can walk to the motel, but I had been planning to drive up to Madison."

"I called the hospital," Katy said. "Boyle is in critical but stable condition."

"I called, too, and heard the same thing. But apparently no one has been up there to collect the evidence."

By evidence, she knew he meant the bullet. "Really? That seems odd."

"I know. It might be that the deputies just haven't been up there yet, but I thought it might be good to see for myself."

Katy nodded slowly. "I could drive you up there," she offered before she could talk herself out of it.

Reese smiled, and her heart did a funny little flip-flop in her chest. "Nice of you to offer, but I'm sure you have better things to do with your free time on your day off."

Sad fact was, she really didn't. She forced a smile and shook her head. "My only plan was to maybe take a hike, and it's far too hot for that. I really don't have any other plans."

Hope filled Reese's hazel-green eyes. "Are you sure? I'd be happy to pay for a tank of gas."

"It's really no bother," she assured him. "And this little car gets great gas mileage, especially compared to your truck." There was no way she was going to allow him to pay for her gas. She was fairly certain DNR game wardens didn't make that much money, and she had more than enough to spare.

"Well, then, thanks, I'd love a ride to Madison."

She had to bite her lip when Reese opened the back passenger door for Duke, who nimbly leaped onto the seat. She shrank back, half expecting him to sniff her again, but she needn't have worried. Duke simply stretched out once again, as if he was right at home.

Was she crazy to drive Reese and his dog to Madison? The drive would take an hour, easily. What on earth would they talk about?

When Reese slid into the passenger seat beside her and clicked his seat belt, she knew it was too late to change her mind.

Katy headed for the highway, trying to think of a safe topic to discuss. "How's your arm?" she asked. "Do we need to stop and pick up your antibiotics?"

"No worries, I have them right here," Reese said, patting his pocket. "My arm hurts, but it's nothing I can't handle. I changed the dressing this morning, and I didn't see any sign of infection."

She nodded, thinking it wouldn't hurt to check his incisions herself, just to be sure. Picking up speed on the highway, she kept a keen eye out for signs for the interstate.

Roughly five miles later, she took the on-ramp and relaxed when she reached freeway speed.

"Do you mind if I ask you a question?" he asked.

Surprised, she glanced at him. "Of course not. What is it?"

"Last night, when you were working on Boyle, why did you step back and let that other guy finish up?"

She shrugged, secretly glad the question wasn't too personal. "He's the trauma surgeon. I'm not."

"So basically, he should have been there right from the beginning. You sent that nurse to go and find him."

Reese Webster was far too perceptive for his own good. "Yes. I wasn't sure if he'd received the page."

"But he should have," Reese pressed.

"Yes, but there are a few dead spots in the hospital, so there's no way to know for sure. Why do you ask?"

"I was just curious. You seemed to have everything under control."

She was glad he thought so, even though, at the time, she'd been scared to death of making a mistake. Glancing in the rearview mirror, she noticed a large black truck coming up behind her at a rapid pace. "What in the world?" she muttered, quickly switching over to the right lane to get out of the way.

The big black truck switched lanes too.

Realization dawned, and her hands tightened on the steering wheel. For a moment, panic seized her by the throat. What should she do?

There weren't many options.

"Hang on," she warned, wrenching the steering wheel to the right and stomping on the brake as she headed off the highway.

R eese saw the black truck coming up fast and quickly dialed 911 on his cell phone. "This is Game Warden Webster. We're being chased by a black truck, license plate number TXR 990, five miles from Highway Double X."

He pressed his feet to the floor as Katy drove off the highway, bouncing over the shoulder and onto the flat grassy area as the car slowed to a stop. Duke yelped behind them, and Reese winced as he heard the dog slide to the floor. He had a crated area in his truck for the dog but obviously didn't have it in Katy's car. Reese spared a quick glance to make sure Duke was okay, and in a heartbeat, the black truck zoomed past them, having way too much momentum to slow down and stop.

Before he could say anything, Katy stomped on the accelerator. The car jerked forward, and Duke let out another yelp. She pulled back onto the freeway, crossed three lanes of thankfully light traffic to find a turnaround where cops sometimes sat to catch speeders. She executed a completely illegal U-turn and headed in the opposite direction.

"Were you a stunt driver before attending medical school?" he asked dryly as his heart returned to a normal rhythm.

Her smile was strained. "No, but maybe I should have been. How's Duke? Is he okay?"

"He'll be fine." Reese could tell she was badly shaken, and he didn't blame her. "I'm sorry, Katy. I suspect the driver of that black truck was after me."

"You don't know that for sure," she protested.

Oh, yes, he did. He scrubbed his hands over his face, regretting the fact that he'd dragged her into this mess. The blond dude must have been watching his truck last night, waiting for him to show up. Otherwise how could he have known which car was Katy's? The idea that they'd been followed made him feel sick to his stomach.

This had to end. Now. Before something else happened.

"Head to the sheriff's department," he said in a low tone. "We'll file a report, and since we have a license plate, there's a good chance they'll find this guy."

"Are you sure you don't want to head to Madison first?" she asked. "We can always report the near miss later."

"No, it's not worth risking your life." He hated thinking about just how close the near miss had been. The way the truck had barreled down at them, he suspected the driver had been planning to hit them in the rear, hoping they'd lose control while he kept going.

Good thing he'd managed to get the license plate number. At least the sheriff's deputies would have something to go on.

Katy was quiet as she drove back toward Crystal Lake and the Hope County Sheriff's Department. He kept sneaking glances at her, wondering if she might break down now that the danger was over.

But he should have known better. She parked the car in the parking lot and jumped out from the driver's seat before he'd even gotten his door open. He quickly lowered the back window for Duke, commanding him to stay, before following her inside.

"Did you hear me?" Katy said, her voice rising with anger. Reese could certainly hear her, so he had to assume the deputy standing in front of her could, too. "I demand to speak to Sheriff Torretti immediately!"

"Calm down, Dr. Katy," one of the deputies said, holding up his hands as if in surrender. "I understand you're upset, but Sheriff Torretti isn't here. He's out of town with his wife. I'm afraid you'll have to make do with me."

Fury radiated from her in waves, and he hid a smile at her redheaded temper as he stepped forward, putting a reassuring hand on her arm. "We'd like to file a police report against the black truck that tried to run us off the road."

"I'm Deputy Ian Kramer," the deputy said, holding out his hand, looking relieved to have someone calm to talk to.

Reese hadn't met this deputy before and reached out to shake his hand. "DNR Game Warden Reese Webster, and I have the license plate number for you. I'd appreciate your cooperation in finding this guy."

"We'd appreciate it," Katy interjected. "It was my car he almost hit."

"I understand. We'll put out a warrant right away," Deputy Kramer assured them.

It didn't take long for the deputy to take down all the details, and Reese tried not to think about the fact that they didn't have much to hold the guy on, if they even found him.

Reckless driving? That was nothing more than a traffic offense.

"There's a few other things I'd like to discuss," Reese said when Katy had finished her story. "Could we go someplace private?"

Deputy Kramer looked surprised and wary, but nodded. "Sure, this way."

The Hope County Sheriff's Department had two small interrogation rooms, and he pulled out a chair for Katy before dropping into the seat beside her. Deputy Kramer sat across from them, eyeing them expectantly.

"As you probably know, I was tracking a poacher who shot a bear and a cougar," Reese said carefully, unsure of how much Kramer actually knew about his case. "When I shouted at Marcus Boyle to stop, he took a shot at me, and I fired back."

Deputy Kramer nodded. "I read Deputy Armbruster's report."

"I forgot to mention that there was a second man I'd seen a few times while tracking Boyle. A tall blond guy, about six feet tall and weighing roughly two hundred pounds. I'd estimate his age to be in his mid-to late-twenties. The way he moved made me think he might have spent time in the military."

Kramer raised a brow. "You think this is the guy who trashed your truck. Which was towed to Billy's, in case you're wondering."

"I know, I was already over there." His truck was beyond repair, at least according to Hank. But right now that was the least of his problems. "I have some evidence linking the poaching to Boyle. After the incident with the bear, I caught a glimpse of the blond guy, but so far I don't have anything to prove he exists. I even thought that maybe Boyle had done the damage to my truck sometime before I caught him shooting the cougar. But after today, I know that it must have been the blond guy since Boyle is still in the hospital."

Kramer nodded. "All right, let's say the blond guy tried to run you off the road. Why? Just for revenge because you caught Boyle? That doesn't seem logical. You'd think Boyle's partner would take off to poach someplace else. There's plenty of wilderness for the guy to use. It makes no sense to keep coming after you."

"I know it's not logical," he admitted. "Unless he's some sort of relative to Boyle. What have you guys found out about him? Does he have family? Brothers? Friends? There has to be some link to the blond guy somewhere."

Kramer sat back in his chair with a heavy sigh. "Boyle's daddy is dead, and he doesn't have any brothers. Obviously, we'll keep digging, but right now we don't have any leads on who this second guy might be."

If he exists at all. The deputy didn't say the words, but he could read the doubt in his expression.

Great. Just great. Reese ground his teeth in frustration. "All right, but I hope you keep looking. This guy tried to seriously hurt us today. In fact, I want protection for Katy. This guy knows what kind of car she drives. It won't be a stretch for him to find her address, too."

Deputy Kramer grimaced and shook his head. "I'm sorry. As much as I'd like to provide Dr. Katy protection, we don't have that kind of manpower. I'll make sure that the deputies do frequent drive-bys though. She lives close enough to town that it won't be hard for us to keep an eye on her."

Drive-bys weren't at all what he had in mind, but what could he say? He didn't exactly have an alternative.

As much as he'd prefer to bunk down in her living room,

it was clear she was afraid of Duke. No matter how much danger she was in, he didn't think she'd allow him to move in with his dog. And he didn't have a car, so he couldn't very well park outside her house.

"I have a question about the bullet that was lodged in Boyle's lung," Katy spoke up. "Have you sent someone to Madison to pick it up?"

"Deputy Armbruster is planning to do that as soon as he has a chance," Deputy Kramer acknowledged. "Look, Dr. Katy, I understand your concern, especially after the scare you just had on the freeway, but I need you to trust us to do our jobs, okay?"

"All right," she agreed with obvious reluctance.

Reese rose to his feet, wishing there was some way to keep Katy safe.

Because the alternative was too painful to contemplate.

KATY DID her best to rein in her frustration as they left the sheriff's department, but it wasn't easy. Her footsteps faltered when she noticed Duke hanging his head out the back window.

"Don't be afraid," Reese murmured, coming up beside her. She liked the feel of his hand in the small of her back a little too much. "If you'd spend more time with him, you'd know there's nothing to worry about."

Despite the soaring temperatures and the sun beating down on their heads, she shivered at the thought of spending time with Duke. "He's the biggest dog I've ever seen in my life."

"And he's probably the best-trained dog you've ever seen in your life, too," Reese argued mildly. "He'll obey me without hesitation. And he'd protect us both with his life."

She sensed Reese was hurt that she was afraid of his dog, but she couldn't bring herself to approach the animal, not even for his sake. "I'm sure you're right, but I think it's best if I take you back to the motel."

"Thanks. We can always walk if that would make you feel better." There was no mistaking the disappointment lining his tone.

"Don't be silly. As long as Duke stays in the back, I'll be fine."

Reese jogged around to open her door for her, and she flashed him a smile before sliding in. No one had ever opened her doors for her, and she suspected Reese's mother had something to do with his gentlemanly manners. On one hand, she was perfectly capable of opening her own doors, but the fact that he cared enough to be polite resonated somewhere deep within.

The last guy she'd dated, Jeff Andrews, had distanced himself in the aftermath of Steffie's death. Even after she'd been exonerated from any wrongdoing, he'd kept his distance. When she'd informed him she was leaving Baltimore General, he'd assured her it was for the best. He'd actually appeared relieved to have her gone.

Looking back, she understood that Jeff had been trying to protect his own reputation in the hospital. But still, he clearly hadn't really cared about her as a woman. Or even as a colleague.

Shaking off the troublesome memories wasn't easy. She glanced over at Reese only to find him watching her intently. She blushed and then mentally bemoaned her fair skin.

"Katy, how would you like to go for a boat ride on the lake?" he asked.

She blinked in surprise. Had she missed something? "You have a boat?"

"Well, actually, Hank has one that he offered to let me use for the day," he explained. "To make up for not having a car ready for me. And the thought of sitting in a motel room doing nothing isn't at all appealing. Please come with me. There's no reason not to enjoy a nice day out on the water."

Katy wanted to say yes, but she couldn't help glancing in the backseat at Duke. "How does Duke like the water?"

Reese flashed a grin. "Actually, he loves it, but I can leave him in the motel room for a few hours."

"Really?" She couldn't keep the relief from her tone. "All right, then I'd be happy to go out in a boat with you."

"Great. Why don't you drop us off and then head home to change into something more comfortable." He gestured lightly to her short-sleeved sweater and flowered skirt that she'd worn to church. "I'll get the boat keys from Hank and meet you back at the motel."

"Sounds good." She pulled into the motel parking lot and kept the car idling while Reese slid out and then opened the door for Duke.

The dog didn't move but waited until Reese said, "Come," before he bounded out of the backseat. Reese flashed her a quick smile. "See you soon."

"All right." After he slammed the door, she put the car in reverse and backed carefully out of the parking space. It wasn't until she was at home, while changing into shorts and a tank top, that she began to doubt the wisdom of spending time with Reese.

Even if she was ready to have a relationship, they would no doubt have completely different schedules to go along with their opposite personalities. She cared for people; he cared about animals. He adored the outdoors while she preferred sitting at home with a good book.

He didn't know anything about the mistakes of her past,

and while he didn't seem the type to judge her unfairly, the fact of the matter was, she still wrestled with guilt.

She'd almost talked herself out of going out on the lake, but the thought of leaving Reese standing at the motel, waiting for her, made her wince. Talk about rude! And going over there just to tell him she'd changed her mind seemed ridiculous. He'd see right through whatever pathetic excuse she came up with, and that would only make him more curious about why she'd backed out of something any number of friends would do.

She stared at her reflection in the mirror. She needed to remember this wasn't a date. They were two adults spending time together, nothing more.

This absolutely wasn't a date.

REESE WAS SWEATING by the time he'd gotten the boat keys from Hank and made his way back to the motel. He risked a quick cold shower before pulling on cargo shorts and a T-shirt. The boat was moored along the public dock, one of the few boats left since most of the others were out on the water.

He was looking forward to relaxing on the lake. Granted, spending the afternoon with Katy was no hardship, either, but he knew he couldn't afford to think of her as anything but a friend.

Any woman who didn't like dogs—or any other animals, for that matter—wasn't for him. Best to remember that fact.

He stopped in at Rose's Cafe, requesting a couple of cold sandwiches to go. Josie's knowing smile made him grimace but even the gossip that would surely follow wasn't enough to stop him. There were already two bottles of water from the vending machine chilling in a bucket of ice in his room.

Katy pulled up mere seconds after he'd returned to the room. "Stay," he said to Duke, who looked forlorn at being left behind. "Guard."

Duke obediently stretched out on the floor, watching him with his dark eyes. Was he crazy to take Katy out on the boat when he could be spending time with his best friend?

As he walked outside, holding their sandwiches and water, the sight of Katy wearing casual shorts and a tank top stole his breath. She was beautiful. No way was he going to regret spending the afternoon with her.

"Hope you don't mind, I brought some food for us," he said as he met up with her. "This way we don't have to hurry back."

Was it his imagination, or was her smile strained? "Sounds great."

"This way," he said, walking down to the community pier. Hank's red speedboat was nothing fancy, but he didn't care. He jumped in and set down the food and water in a small hollowed out area in the bow and then went back to give Katy a hand.

"You know what you're doing, right?" she asked, looking a bit apprehensive.

"Absolutely. I used to own a boat of my own." He didn't add that he'd had to sell it at a loss when Suzanne had cleaned out their joint bank account. He'd managed to get enough for the boat to cover the outstanding loan, leaving nothing extra.

Katy sat down in the seat next to the pilot's chair, watching as he disconnected the moor lines and then started the engine. He put the throttle in reverse and carefully backed away from the pier.

He putt-putted across the no wake zone and then gave it a little gas when they passed the buoys.

"Wow, this is amazing!" Katy exclaimed as the wind whipped at her hair. She once again wore it back in the fancy braid she favored, and he found himself wishing she'd wear it long and unbound for him. Although it was hardly practical while out on the boat.

"Hang on," he said, pushing the throttle forward. The front of the boat leaped up and bounced against the waves. He grinned and steered clear of a boat pulling an inner tube with a swimmer riding inside it.

He pulled back on the throttle, slowing down so he could make a circle around the lake. When he glanced over at Katy, she looked dazed yet happy.

"That was fun," she declared. "I like going fast."

"Me, too. But there are a lot of boats out, so we can't let her rip too much."

"I know; it's crazy busy out here." A shadow darkened her eyes. "I hope the ER doesn't get slammed."

"I'm sure they can handle it, just like you do when you're on." There was a boat coming toward them, so he cranked the wheel to get out of the way.

But the boat didn't move off course. He laid on the horn and pushed up the throttle, trying to get out of the way. At the last possible moment, the boat sped past, missing them by inches.

The boat rocked crazily against the wake, and he pulled back the throttle, glaring over at the careless driver. The boat was heading in the opposite direction now, but he could easily see the broad-shouldered man driving it.

A man with close-cropped blond hair.

5

When Reese hit the gas, Katy swallowed a shriek and clutched the edge of the boat, silently praying for safety, relieved when the boat swept past, missing them by inches.

"Did you get a good look at that guy?" Reese asked harshly.

"No, why? Did he look familiar?"

"I don't know. Maybe." Reese grimaced and shook his head. "He had blond hair, but so do dozens of other people on the lake."

She realized he thought the boat driver might be the same guy who'd tried to crash into them earlier. Seemed unlikely, though. How would some stranger figure out that Reese had rented a boat from Hank? A car, maybe, but a boat? "Does Hank lend out this boat often?" she asked.

"Sometimes, but not often," Reese said. "You're right, though, it doesn't make sense that the blond dude just happened to follow us onto the lake."

"It's not impossible," she mused. "Do you think we should report this to Deputy Kramer?"

"Nah, I didn't get the ID number from the boat, and unfortunately, the guy is long gone. For all we know, this was nothing more than some tourist looking for a thrill." The dark shadow in his eyes made her think he'd only tacked on that last statement for her benefit.

"Maybe we should head back," she murmured.

There was a long silence while he steered the boat off into a small cove where there weren't many other boats. When he killed the motor, he turned to look at her with a smile. "I promised you a picnic, so why don't we drop anchor here and eat?"

Since she didn't really want to leave—being out on the boat was so much nicer than being stuck at home—she nodded. "All right."

"Great. Just give me a minute." Reese pulled the anchor out from beneath the bench seat and dropped it over the side. She was surprised at how he seemed to ignore the wound in his left arm. Surely it had to still hurt? He wore a T-shirt today, and it looked like a fresh gauze strip had been wrapped around his arm.

"Seems like you're the type to have a boat of your own," she said, watching him move around with confidence. "You obviously know what you're doing."

He froze for a moment and then shrugged. "Boats cost money, and I work too much to make the investment worthwhile." He avoided her gaze as he pulled up the short canopy to provide some shade. Maybe it was her imagination, but he seemed tense. Or maybe defensive. "You should sit under here so you don't burn."

"Believe me, I lathered up with sunscreen, but thanks." She took the seat directly beneath the canopy, wondering if she'd made him mad. Was he sensitive about money? She had no idea how much DNR game wardens made, but surely he didn't have too many bills living alone.

Not that it was any of her business. She waited as Reese pulled out the sandwiches, chips and two bottles of water.

"I hope you don't mind turkey on whole wheat," he said, handing her a wrapped package. "I wasn't sure what you liked, so I took a guess based on the chicken sandwich you had last night."

"Turkey on whole wheat is exactly what I would have ordered," she assured him. "Why? What do you have?"

"Roast beef." When he grinned, he looked younger, more carefree, and she decided her imagination had been working overtime earlier. Right now, Reese Webster looked as if he didn't have a care in the world, despite being shot in the arm by a poacher. "But if you didn't like turkey, I would have traded."

She laughed and bit into her sandwich, suddenly starving. "Guess today is your lucky day."

"Absolutely," he agreed, and his intense gaze made her wonder if he was talking about being out with her, rather than the sandwich.

She told herself to get a grip. They were friends helping each other out. Nothing more. Averting her gaze, she looked out over the lake, amazed to realize it was actually much larger than she'd originally thought. And so many people. Kids and adults alike were tubing, skiing and playing around on Jet Skis. There were even a few kids swimming, but they were on a floaty thing closer to shore, well out of the way from the motorized toys.

"Is this your first boat ride?" Reese asked.

She grimaced. "Is it that obvious? Yes, this is my first boat ride. I grew up in the city, and even though Baltimore is on the coast, I never had the opportunity to go out on the ocean."

"Crystal Lake is way different than being out on the ocean," Reese said dryly. "The waves get pretty choppy out in the Atlantic."

"Did you live on the ocean?" she asked, curious about Reese's life. He'd mentioned not having any family, no one to worry about him, but she sensed right now he was speaking from experience.

A smile tugged at the corner of his mouth. "I did live on the ocean. On a boat in the ocean." At her puzzled glance, he clarified. "I did a four-year stint in the navy."

"And here I thought your mother drilled those manners into you," she teased. "I should have guessed you spent time in the military."

"Oh, my mother expected manners too," he said dryly. "She's been gone for three years, but I'm sure I'd hear her chiding me if I didn't keep up what she taught."

"I'm sorry for your loss," she said. "Cancer?"

"Brain aneurysm." The words came out clipped. "We were told to be happy she went quickly and didn't suffer." His expression told her what he thought about that idea.

"I'm sorry," she repeated, understanding this topic was treading on shaky ground. She knew from dealing with patients that sometimes the abrupt deaths were the most difficult just because they were so unexpected. Most families grieved about being unable to say good-bye. "I'm sure that was very difficult for you and your family. I hope you can find a little comfort in knowing she's in a much better place now."

He raised an eyebrow and shrugged. "Maybe. Once I might have believed that, although I'm not so sure anymore."

She didn't know what had happened to cause him to lose his faith, but she sensed he had secrets. But what difference did it make? So did she. For a moment, she sat back, wondering if this was the reason that God had thrown Reese into her path.

To help him rediscover his faith.

A mission she couldn't refuse.

REESE FINISHED HIS FOOD, searching for a way to change the subject. How had they gone from sharing a picnic to talking about death? Not exactly a good topic for spending the afternoon on the lake.

"Do you want to swim?" he asked. "I can't because of the stitches, but you could."

She laughed and shook her head. "I don't think so. I didn't bring a swimming suit."

Her laugh made her look innocent, a far cry from the determined doctor he'd watched perform surgery on Boyle. It was difficult to ignore Katy's beauty, the way her hair came loose from her braid, trailing around her face, and her cheeks turning pink from the sun.

"Well, then, I guess we'll do another swing around the lake before heading in." Strange how he didn't want this day to end. Normally he preferred spending time alone, hiking in the woods with no one but Duke for company. His buddies called him a hermit, and maybe that was partially true. He didn't particularly care for crowds, but it was also easier to save money when you didn't go out or do anything for fun.

In fact, the money he'd spent today, gas for the boat and their modest lunch, was the first money he'd spent on something frivolous since Suzanne had left him.

He waited for the flash of guilt, but it never came. Even knowing he'd have to come up with the cash for the deductible on his insurance didn't make him regret the money he'd spent today.

"Here, let me," Katy said, taking the wrapping and napkins from his hands. Their fingers brushed, sending a little zip up his arm.

"I'll get the anchor then," he muttered, edging around her to the bow of the boat. By the time he had the anchor pulled up and the canopy down, she had all the garbage tucked away in a neat little bag.

"Thanks for the picnic," she said. "And for the boat ride."

"You're welcome. Hang on." He pushed the throttle forward, steering the boat back out to the center of the lake.

Katy put her hand up to shade her eyes as she gazed out at the skiers. He'd love to get her up on skis and wondered if she'd be willing. Not now, but maybe in a few weeks or so.

Wait a minute, what was he thinking? This wasn't a date. This was just a way to say thank you for the way she'd helped him out.

"Reese, hurry! Look over there! That boy is having trouble."

Her shout pushed his thoughts aside, and he squinted in the direction she pointed. He caught sight of a kid who looked to be about ten years old, floundering in the water. He cranked the wheel and pushed the speed as far as he dared to reach the boy.

"He's under! Hurry!" Before he realized what she intended to do, she kicked off her shoes and climbed up along the side of the boat.

"Wait, I'll go," he called, but it was too late. Katy dove into the water.

He pulled back the throttle, trying to come up alongside the spot where he'd last seen the child. The lake was murky, mostly from all the mud that had been churned up from the boat motors. He held his breath until Katy's head broke the surface in roughly the spot where they'd seen the boy go down.

She took another deep breath and then went back down in the water. How in the world she'd find the kid was beyond him. He struggled to come up with another plan, but if he dove into the water, who would manage the boat? No, he couldn't risk it.

Suddenly, the boy surfaced, waving his arms frantically.

"Over here!" Reese called, pulling out the round life-saver. He tossed it toward the boy, but the kid was too panicked and abruptly sank back down beneath the surface again.

"Come on, come on," he urged under his breath. And for the first time in years, he sent up a silent prayer.

Lord, please save him! Save them both!

After what seemed like an eternity, two heads broke the surface of the water, and he felt an overwhelming relief. Katy had the child, but he soon realized the boy was limp, as if he was unconscious.

Not dead. Please, Lord, not dead!

"Grab the life preserver. I'll pull you in." Reese knew they had to move quickly.

Katy grabbed ahold of the life preserver and used it to help keep the boy's head above water. Reese slowly pulled them in, amazed to see that she was trying to do mouth-to-mouth resuscitation right there in the water. It couldn't have been easy, but somehow she was making it work.

"Help me get him up," she gasped when he pulled them

to the edge of the boat. He flipped the ladder down and leaned over the side to grasp the boy beneath his arms. The kid was light, so it didn't take much to yank him out of the water.

He put the boy down on the floor of the boat while Katy climbed in. Water poured off her in tiny streams as she came over to kneel beside the boy. He swallowed hard as she pressed her fingers to the child's neck. "He has a pulse, but we need to get the water out of his lungs."

Reese nodded. "I can help. Tell me what you want me to do."

"Just keep his head turned to the side." She straddled the boy and performed several abdominal thrusts. Then she went back to try and give more mouth-to-mouth breathing, forcing air into his lungs.

Abruptly, the boy started choking, and she quickly rolled him over on his side just in time for him to throw up all the water he'd swallowed. He continued to cough and gag, struggling for air while Katy quietly reassured him.

Once Reese saw that the boy was okay, he stepped over them to take the wheel. Now that he was paying attention to the other people on the lake, he could see there was a boat barreling down on them. Not the blond dude, but several people crowded around, looking anxious.

"Jacob! Are you okay?" one of them called.

"Are those your parents?" he asked.

"My friend's parents," the kid mumbled. "They're gonna be mad at me 'cause I told them I could swim."

Reese met Katy's concerned gaze over the boy's head. She put her arm around the boy's bony shoulders and gave him a reassuring squeeze. "First of all, they're going to be happy that you're okay. But you shouldn't have lied to them,

Jacob. Not about something this important. You almost drowned today."

"I know," Jacob said, his tiny body shaking now that the immediate threat was over. He sniffled loudly. "I'm sorry about the mess on your boat, mister."

Reese flashed the boy a warm smile. "Hey, don't worry about it, I'll get it cleaned up in no time."

"Jacob? What happened?" A woman called out as the boat slid alongside them. "Are you all right?"

"He's fine," Katy assured them. "But he should probably be checked out at the hospital, just to be sure. I'm afraid he inhaled quite a bit of water."

"I'm sorry," Jacob said, hanging his head low. "I should have been wearing a life jacket the way you told me to."

"Yes, you should have, but right now, I'm just thankful you're all right." The woman flashed a grateful smile at Katy. "You look familiar," she said. "My name is Andrea Walters."

"I'm Dr. Katy Reichert. I work in the Hope County ER."

"Lucky for us you were here to help Jacob," Andrea said with a smile. "When we realized he'd fallen in, we swung around but couldn't see him. I'm so glad you were able to find him."

"It's no problem." Katy reached over to hold the boats together so Jacob could get across. The family welcomed him by wrapping him in a towel and then plunking a life jacket over his head and tying it securely.

Katy pushed the boat away and turned back to face Reese. "Do you have a towel, by chance?" she asked, trying to wring out her soaked clothing.

"Right here." He pulled a towel out, and she took it gratefully.

"Well, that was an exciting end to our picnic," she said, pulling the towel across her shoulders and crossing the ends in front of her chest. "Although I wouldn't have minded skipping the water rescue part."

"Once again, you were amazing," he said as he turned the boat toward the community pier. "I nearly had heart failure when you jumped in. Why didn't you let me do it?"

"Did you forget about your stitches? Besides, I don't know how to steer a boat."

Maybe he had forgotten the stupid stitches, but that wouldn't have held him back from trying to rescue the boy. "You must have lifeguard training."

"No, just instincts." She sighed. "But that was too close. I couldn't see anything in the water, and I was so afraid I wouldn't be able to save him. All I could do was pray."

"I prayed too." The words popped out of his mouth before he could stop them.

Katy's quick smile made him feel like a fraud. Just because he'd prayed in a time of crisis didn't mean he was a reformed Christian or anything.

"God is always there for us, Reese," Katy said softly. Even with her matted-down hair and soaking-wet clothes, she still looked beautiful. "No matter what may have happened in the past. I hope you give Him another chance."

"I'll try," was the extent of what he was willing to commit to.

She smiled again, and he forced himself to concentrate on what he was doing. He knew better than to encourage her. Why had he even suggested this picnic in the first place? It wasn't as if he could offer her anything more than friendship. There was no way he could risk getting involved in another relationship. Not when his job required him to be gone for long hours at a time. Maybe it wasn't as long as the stints he'd pulled in the navy, but long enough.

Katy was smart, talented, and a doctor, for heaven's sake.

She saved people's lives every day. Even if he was in the market for a relationship, she was way out of his reach. She deserved far better than a loner who was up to his eyeballs in debt.

The sooner his brain got that message, the better.

6

"Are you sure you don't want me to drop you off at your house?" Reese asked.

Katy shook her head. "As much as I'd like that, there isn't a pier over there. I guess I'd rather not wade through the muck to get on land."

"All right."

She watched as Reese deftly maneuvered the boat along the community pier. Walking back to her house wouldn't take too long, although she knew her appearance would make people curious enough to stare and ask questions. The hardest thing to get used to in Crystal Lake was the way everyone knew everyone else's business.

"I'd offer you my motel room, but I don't have clothes that would fit you," Reese said apologetically.

Had he figured out what she was thinking? She really needed to work on her poker face. "It's not a big deal. Think of the possible rumors. Maybe the citizens of Crystal Lake will assume you tossed me in the water after I broke things off with you."

He chuckled. "Now there's a thought. Or maybe you

were so upset by our breakup that you jumped in the water on purpose."

She wrinkled her nose at him. "Anyone who knows me wouldn't believe that for a minute."

He opened his mouth as if he were about to say something but then must have thought better of it. "Do you want me to walk you home?"

"No need," she responded hastily. "But maybe I should help you clean up the mess first."

"No, just head home to change your clothes," he said firmly. "Duke can keep me company while I clean this up."

She nodded and told herself she was *not* afraid of Reese's dog. But the animal was a reminder that they were friends and nothing more. "All right. Thanks again for the picnic and boat ride."

"You're welcome." He didn't meet her eyes as he helped her off the boat. She was halfway to her house before she realized she still had his towel.

She made a mental note to make sure to get it back to him as soon as she'd washed it. Not that he probably cared one way or the other about a beach towel.

Was she looking for an excuse to see him again? No, absolutely not.

But after she showered and changed, she put a small load of laundry in the washing machine, including the towel and her smelly lake clothes.

Better to return the stupid towel than to keep it as some sort of memento of their afternoon together.

As the afternoon wore on, the weather grew more stifling, to the point that cooking dinner was not a viable option. She was almost out of fresh veggies too, so she couldn't even throw together a salad.

There was an old-fashioned ice cream parlor on Main Street, unfortunately a little too close to the Crystal Lake Motel for comfort. But was she really going to sit here just to avoid Reese? Talk about ridiculous. For all she knew, he was probably back out on the boat, with Duke for company.

She left her house and walked toward town, cringing at the number of people crowding the sidewalks. Not that she should complain—Crystal Lake depended on tourism for a good portion of its financial stability. Summer was the high point, but they saw good business during the fall festival and hunting season. They were even blessed to have tourists come to cross-country ski and snowmobile in the winter.

No doubt the hunting season was the busiest for Reese and the rest of the DNR game wardens. Although she hadn't realized poaching was such a problem until Reese had first shown up in the ER after being clawed by a wounded bear.

She was so lost in her thoughts that she almost went right past the ice cream parlor. Even though she hadn't eaten dinner yet, she decided there was no reason she couldn't start with dessert. When she pushed open the door, a tiny bell jangled, announcing her arrival.

"Hi, Dr. Katy." The young girl across the counter greeted her with familiarity, and she stared for a minute, trying to place the dark hair pulled back in a ponytail. Oh, yes, she was the young girl who'd come in a few months ago with that nasty flu bug. "Hi, Claire, how are you?"

"I heard you pulled Jacob out of the lake," Claire said, her eyes wide with awe. "Timmy's parents said he would have *died* if you hadn't been there."

"Well, I'm just glad he's okay," Katy said, trying to focus

on the various flavors of ice cream. "What's the special today?"

"You just missed Mr. Webster and his dog," Claire went on as if she hadn't heard the question. "Mr. Webster wouldn't buy anything for Duke, though. He said people food would make him sick."

Good grief, had the rumor mill been so busy that even a high school kid thought they were dating? "I'm sure Mr. Webster knows what's best for his dog, but I think I'd like a dish of the mint chocolate chip, please."

This time, Claire heard the order and busied herself with scooping the ice cream into a small plastic dish. The way Claire looked at her expectantly made her think the girl figured she wanted to catch up with Reese and Duke.

Irrationally, that's exactly what she wanted to do.

Stop it!

She pulled her wallet out of her purse and paid Claire before taking her ice cream. When she left the parlor, she decided to head away from the central part of town where the band was playing, assuming that's where Reese and Duke had been headed. She didn't think having Duke would slow him down, not after the way he'd trained the dog to listen.

The cool ice cream tasted wonderful, and she savored the minty flavor as she meandered away from the congestion of tourists. She headed toward the hilly area where the hiking trail began. Not that she intended to hike, but there was a small bench near the base of the hill.

The moment she sat down, she heard voices and tried not to show her disappointment. So much for having a brief moment of peace and quiet.

"Yeah, you're right, I should just forget about it."

The deep male voice sounded familiar, but she was sure that it was nothing more than her imagination.

A moment later, Reese and Duke emerged from the hiking trail. When he saw her sitting there, he looked guilty about something.

"Hi," Reese greeted her awkwardly.

She hid her smile behind a spoon of ice cream. "Were you really talking to your dog?" she asked.

He lifted a shoulder and nodded. "Why not? Duke is a good listener, aren't you, boy?"

Duke perked up his ears and wagged his tail but didn't come over to sniff at her. Instead, he stayed right beside Reese, almost as if guarding his owner from some potential threat. She had the odd thought that it might be nice to have a pet to keep the loneliness at bay.

But even if she did break down to get a pet, it wouldn't be a dog with huge teeth like Duke.

She pushed the idea away, knowing that having a pet with her crazy schedule was out of the question. "So, how come you're not in town, enjoying the band? I figured you'd make the most of your time here." Every weekend a band set up outside, weather permitting, to play for the tourists.

"Nah, too crowded." He stood for a minute, his hand tucked into the pockets of his cargo shorts. He had nice, tanned legs and was wearing a T-shirt that clung to his broad, muscular shoulders. And why was she noticing that, anyway?

"Why aren't you listening to the band?" he asked, turning her question back on her.

Since she could hardly tell him how she'd come this way to avoid running into him, she shrugged. "Country music isn't my thing."

"I thought I heard a rock-and-roll song a few minutes ago," Reese said with a puzzled frown.

"Oh, country rock, whatever." She concentrated on scraping the last bit of ice cream from the dish. "I hope it didn't take you too long to clean off the boat," she said, rising to her feet.

He waved it off. "No worries. I made sure the boat was cleaner than when Hank loaned it to me. And he thinks he'll have a car available by tomorrow afternoon, too."

For some reason, the thought of Reese leaving town to return to his isolated home tucked into the woods made her feel depressed. Which was completely ridiculous. She should be glad that she wouldn't be tripping over him every time she walked down Main Street.

"Good news for both of you," she said, nodding toward Duke. "I'm sure he misses being able to run around in your backyard."

"Trust me, he does. When I call him into the motel room, I swear he gives me a look full of doggy reproach."

She couldn't help but laugh. "I bet." She hated the fact that she was still intimidated by the massive beast. Even though he was an extremely well-behaved massive beast. "Well, I should really head home. Nice chatting with you."

"Sure. Take care," Reese said, matching her offhand tone.

She turned to leave and didn't think it was an accident that Reese stayed right where he was, with Duke by his side. Was the thought of walking with her too abhorrent? She mentally rolled her eyes. No, she was being stupid. Most likely he was trying to give her space. Plus, he seemed to know she was more than a little afraid of Duke.

Okay, so Reese allowing her to walk home alone was his

way of being polite. So why was she feeling so upset and disconcerted?

She took a deep breath and let it out slowly. But even as she walked away, it took every ounce of will she possessed not to turn around to see him one last time.

REESE KEPT his hand by his side, wordlessly telling Duke to stay right beside him since he sensed the dog wanted to follow Katy.

Or maybe Duke was just picking up on his desire to follow Katy.

Reminding himself over and over again that this was for the best didn't make him feel any better. He hadn't gone too far up the hiking trail, mostly because dusk was falling and he didn't want to risk losing his footing on unfamiliar terrain.

Having a gunshot wound in his arm was one thing. Being stupid enough to sprain an ankle would be far worse. His boss was already chomping at the bit for him to get back to work.

So far, Gavin hadn't found the dead cougar, either. They'd had no trouble finding the kill site—there had been plenty of blood marking the spot, so that wasn't the problem. Granted, it was possible a scavenger had dragged it away, but there should be signs of that, too. According to Gavin, he and George had been combing the woods all day but still hadn't found so much as a tuft of fur.

Reese knew with sick certainty that they would never find the cougar because the blond dude had already scooped it up. There was no other explanation for how the carcass had disappeared without a trace.

Taking the bullet evidence with it.

After waiting a good fifteen minutes, he began to walk back toward town. He was extremely grateful that he would only need to stay one more night at the motel. And not just because of the added expense. The noise from people going up and down Main Street at all hours of the night was driving him crazy.

Thinking about the lost evidence from the cougar made him even more anxious to talk to the sheriff's deputies again. They'd get the bullet from Boyle's chest and match it to his gun, but so far, he didn't have as much evidence against Boyle as he would have liked. He had his eyewitness account, sure. And the photos of the boot prints he'd found, along with the bullet from the bear.

Would that be enough? He sincerely hoped so.

Without conscious thought, he ended up outside the sheriff's department headquarters, located a little outside of town. But, of course, the place was shut down to the public this late on a Sunday night.

He considered banging on the door to get the dispatcher's attention but figured the deputies would be busy.

As he turned to leave, a deputy vehicle pulled up and stopped beside him. The deputy rolled down his window, and he recognized Armbruster. "Webster, right?"

"Yeah, that's right."

"Your dog should be on a leash," Armbruster said with a frown.

"He's trained as a police dog. He won't do anything without a command from me." Reese kept his voice even, but he was getting annoyed with this deputy.

"He still needs to be on a leash," Armbruster repeated. "What are you doing here, anyway? Did you need something?"

"Just wanted to check up on where you're at with the

investigation." Reese wished he hadn't come this way since he suspected Armbruster wouldn't tell him anything, even if he had some news.

"No news yet, but we're working on it."

"Okay, thanks." Reese moved as if to leave.

"Heard you and Dr. Katy saved that boy this afternoon," Armbruster said. "Nice work."

He shouldn't have been surprised at how fast news traveled through Crystal Lake, but he was. "Thanks, but Dr. Katy is the one who did the work. I just helped."

"We're lucky to have Dr. Katy working here. She's a very talented lady," Armbruster agreed.

Reese nodded, understanding the unspoken warning. Armbruster didn't want him doing anything to hurt their beloved doctor. And he understood; he would feel the same way. "See you later, Deputy." He lifted his hand in a wave and then turned around to head back toward the motel. Duke, thankfully, behaved himself by walking directly at his side the entire way.

"Don't look at me like that," he said to Duke as he unlocked the door. "I don't like it here anymore than you do."

Duke huffed and crossed the threshold, leaving Reese to do the same. A group of giggling kids walked by, their shrill voices piercing the night air.

Reese sighed and shut the door behind him. This was going to be a long night, in more ways than one.

KATY STARED at the ceiling fan swirling over her bed, trying to figure out why she couldn't fall asleep.

As much as she wanted to blame Reese, she was more tuned in to every little creak and groan of the house. Normal sounds that, for some reason, had never bothered her before.

She closed her eyes and prayed, seeking peace. The church services she'd attended earlier that morning seemed like days ago rather than hours. But instead of remembering Pastor John's sermon, the image of Jacob's still features flashed in her memory.

For a moment, he'd reminded her painfully of Steffie. The young girl had been several years older than Jacob, but her pale, lifeless face had haunted Katy for the past year.

She squeezed her eyes shut and tried to find comfort in the fact that Jacob hadn't died. God had spared his life today.

Why hadn't he spared Steffie's?

To teach her a lesson. To make her realize that she needed to pay more attention to her patients' signs and symptoms. To remind her that patients were people who needed care, not just to be shuffled through the revolving door that the Baltimore General ED had become.

Her chest tightened with guilt, and she blinked back the tears. If she could take back that night she'd discharged Steffie without requesting a surgical consult, she would. But Steffie's pain had gone away after she'd given a fluid bolus, so she hadn't considered appendicitis as a probable cause of the pain, especially since she'd had a waiting room full of patients still to be seen.

And when Steffie's parents had brought her back to the ER four days later, after her appendix had burst, it had been too late. Steffie had died of massive sepsis.

I'm sorry. I'm so sorry! Dear Lord, please forgive me. Please!

Somehow, she must have dozed because a muffled thud woke her up. For a moment, she peered through the darkness, wondering if her mind was playing tricks on her again. Was probably nothing, just someone slamming a car door.

A creak from a floorboard made her sit bolt upright in bed. She recognized that creak from the center of her living room.

Someone was in her house!

7

Katy grabbed her cell phone that she thankfully kept on the bedside table next to her—just in case the hospital needed to get ahold of her—and disconnected it from the charger. Then she slipped out of bed, down onto the floor, hiding behind the bed as she quickly considered her options. The bed was between her and the doorway, and the bathroom was also near the doorway, far too close to the living room.

She had no intention of going anywhere near where the intruder was. Which meant she was trapped.

What should she do? The only thing on this side of the bedroom was a small, barely-able-to-walk-in closet and a window that led to the back of the house.

She could maybe hide in the closet at least long enough to call 911.

The better answer was to go out the window, but she was afraid she'd make too much noise. What if the intruder heard her leave? If he had a gun, he could shoot her from the doorway. The image made her shudder.

No, she should probably call the authorities first and plot her escape later.

Staying low, she crawled on her hands and knees toward the closet. The door was ajar, so she soundlessly opened it farther and eased inside before carefully closing it behind her.

Not the best hiding spot—it wouldn't take long for the intruder to find her—so she needed to act quickly. Slipping a heavy sweater off one of the hangers, she cupped it around her head and the phone in an effort to muffle the noise as she dialed 911.

The phone rang five times on the other end, making her want to scream in frustration before a dispatcher answered. "Please state the nature of your emergency," the woman said in what seemed like an unnecessarily loud voice.

Was the sweater enough to muffle the sound? Or could the intruder hear her? Sweat beaded on her forehead, and she tried not to shake.

"This is Dr. Katy," she whispered. "Someone's in my house."

That got the dispatcher's attention as her voice went quiet. "I have a deputy nearby," the dispatcher said softly. "Stay on the line with me while I send him over."

One good thing about small towns: everyone knew where everyone else lived, so she didn't have to risk telling the dispatcher what her address was. She was already afraid she'd been too loud. Tucking the phone in the folds of the sweater, she leaned forward and placed her ear near the closet door, straining to listen.

There was nothing but silence.

Did that mean the intruder was gone? Was this her chance to escape? Should she make a run for the window?

Or stay put? And if the person was still in her house, why was it suddenly so quiet?

An insidious frisson of doubt crept in as she stayed huddled in the closet. Had she imagined the creaking floorboard? Would the deputy get here and find nothing amiss? She'd feel ridiculous if that was the case, but she was too frightened to open the closet door to look.

Better to be considered a hysterical female than to risk being attacked by a would-be rapist.

Now she was letting her imagination run wild. Rapists didn't run around in small towns like Crystal Lake. Did they?

She reached up to open the closet door when she heard the floorboard creak again. The sound was so loud she knew it hadn't been her imagination. Her heart raced as she thought about what she had in her closet that might be used as a weapon. A coat hanger? Maybe, but the intruder would have to get close for that to be effective, and if he had a gun, she'd be toast.

Too bad she didn't have a baseball bat or some other heavy object.

A book? Hope filled her chest as she remembered storing some of her heavy medical textbooks on the shelf that stretched across the rack of clothes. Throwing a pathophysiology book at him could potentially buy her the few seconds necessary to escape.

Maybe.

Maybe not. Who was she kidding?

Since she couldn't think of another plan, she pushed the sweater-wrapped phone aside, knowing that it would be useless if the intruder found her anyway. Feeling her way in the pitch-black closet wasn't easy, but she forced herself to remember what the items in her closet looked like as she carefully stood. Avoiding the hangers so they wouldn't clang together wasn't easy. Still, she stretched up to feel along the top edge of the shelf.

Inch by inch, she moved her hands until she felt the cardboard box of books. Reaching up, she felt the box's dimensions, making sure it was the right one. She remembered just how heavy the box had been when she'd placed it up there after moving in.

Still, she needed to do something. Imagining the intruder coming into the bedroom was enough to make her lift the box so it wouldn't scrape along the shelf, the muscles in her arms straining with the effort. She pulled it down and swallowed a grunt as she nearly staggered under the weight. She set the box on the floor, grateful for the carpeting, and quickly pulled out one of the heavy textbooks.

Holding it to her chest, she melted back in the corner, wincing as the clothes rustled a bit. She held her breath for another long moment, trying to gauge where the intruder might be. Still in her living room? Or was he making his way through her bedroom?

The wail of sirens split the air, and there was a loud crash as something hit the floor. Katy sucked in a harsh breath, her heart pounding so hard she could barely hear.

She had no idea how long she sat in the closet clutching her textbook, but it seemed like forever before she heard a deep male voice calling her name.

"Katy? Katy! Where are you?"

Maybe her ears were playing more tricks on her because she could have sworn that the voice belonged to Reese. She pushed open the closet door at the same moment that lights flooded her bedroom.

"I'm here," she said, inwardly wincing at her weak voice. It took a minute for her eyes to adjust to the bright lights, but she squinted enough to see Reese and Duke standing just inside her bedroom. She cleared her throat and rose to her feet. "I'm fine."

"Dr. Katy?" She heard Deputy Kramer's voice in the living room and realized he must have been a few steps behind Reese. How Reese and his dog had managed to get here first, she had no clue. "You should have waited for me, Webster," the deputy said in a low furious tone. "Rushing in here like that, you're lucky you weren't killed."

"Duke needed to go out, and I saw the intruder leaving a few seconds after you set off your sirens," Reese said, raking his gaze over her as if to reassure himself she was okay. "I was more worried about what might have happened to Katy than about being shot."

"I should arrest you for obstruction of justice," Deputy Kramer muttered darkly. He glanced at her with obvious concern. "Dr. Katy, are you sure you're all right?" When she nodded, he smiled. "Why don't you come into the living room so you can tell us what might be missing?"

"Okay," she said, taking a deep breath to calm her racing heart. But her feet remained rooted to the floor after Deputy Kramer left the room.

"Pathophysiology?" Reese asked with a raised eyebrow. "A little light reading for when you're trapped in the closet by a prowler?"

"More like it was the heaviest thing I had in the closet to throw at him," she corrected, tossing the book on her bed, refusing to feel embarrassed. She crossed her arms across her chest, belatedly realizing she was wearing only her nightgown. Feeling self-conscious, she turned back toward the closet to search for her robe.

While she pulled on the lightweight garment, she felt Reese come up to stand behind her. "Are you really all right?" he asked in a low tone. "I was worried sick about you."

Tying the belt of the robe, she turned to face him, relieved to see that Duke was sitting calmly where he'd been standing before rather than following Reese. "I was scared, but I'm fine."

For a moment, he just looked down at her, and then abruptly, he pulled her close, wrapping his arms around her in a fierce hug. She could hear the rapid beat of his heart beneath her ear and understood he'd been as scared as she was.

She leaned against him, savoring the strength of his arms surrounding her. The fact that Reese had actually seen the prowler made the whole incident that much more frightening.

Finally, she pushed herself away, at least far enough to look up into his eyes. "Thanks for coming to my rescue," she said softly.

He nodded and then lowered his head toward hers, covering her mouth with his in a kiss that made her legs feel like jelly. She wrapped her arms around his waist, savoring his kiss.

But the brief moment of intimacy was over far too soon. When Reese lifted his head, she gasped for breath and would have pulled his head down again for a repeat performance if not for the fact that Deputy Kramer chose that moment to call her name.

"Dr. Katy? Are you ready to inventory what might be missing?"

With a sigh of regret, she pulled out of Reese's arms, feeling the loss keenly before she turned to head into the living room. She gave Duke a wide berth, although he didn't move from the spot where he was sitting, despite the way his gaze followed her. As she crossed the threshold, she abruptly stopped, unprepared for the mess that greeted her.

Drawers had been pulled open, the contents disturbed as if someone had been searching for something. Books and her personal papers were also strewn about.

"I don't understand," she said, trying to absorb what had transpired. "What on earth was that guy looking for?"

Deputy Kramer sighed and shook his head. "We were hoping you could tell us."

Katy spread her hands helplessly. "I don't know! My television is still here, and so is my laptop computer. I don't keep anything of value, other than some of my grandmother's jewelry, which is in the bedroom."

"I guess it's possible the sirens scared him off before he could search the bedroom," Deputy Kramer said thoughtfully.

But Reese was shaking his head. "I think it's the same blond dude. The one who trashed my truck and tried to run us off the road."

"You mean the second poacher who no one has seen but you?" Deputy Kramer asked dryly.

Reese scowled and nodded. "Yeah, I know it sounds crazy, but I'm willing to bet that once Boyle regains consciousness, he'll be more than happy to turn on the blond guy in exchange for a lighter sentence. And have you forgotten my smashed truck? I was in the hospital. There's no reason for me to trash my own mode of transportation."

"Last I heard, Boyle was still in the ICU connected to a ventilator," Deputy Kramer said in a slow, deliberate tone. "And for all we know, he smashed your truck hours before you shot him."

Reese gaped at him. "You can't be serious."

Deputy Kramer shrugged. "Awfully convenient that there isn't anyone to challenge your story, isn't it?"

Katy glanced between the two men, trying to understand what was going on. It was late, almost two thirty in the morning, and she wasn't in the mood for games. "What are you talking about, Ian?" she asked. "Why wouldn't you believe a respected game warden like Reese?"

Ian Kramer turned to look at her. "How do you know that this isn't all some elaborate scheme to throw suspicion elsewhere? What if Webster is the one actually doing the poaching? I hear some people will pay a pretty penny for bear and cougar hides."

"Don't be ridiculous. Why would Reese do something like that?" she asked in exasperation. She glanced at Reese, a little nervous at the grim expression on his face.

"Maybe because he has massive debts?" Deputy Kramer said in a snide tone. "From what I saw, he has plenty of motive."

She blinked in shock and looked over at Reese, waiting for him to deny the allegation.

But he didn't. Instead, he turned away. "Come, Duke," he said. The dog hurried after him as he left.

And she didn't think it was an accident that the door loudly banged shut behind him.

REESE'S GUT churned with a mixture of anger and hopelessness as he walked back toward the motel. He shouldn't have been surprised that the sheriff's deputies had performed a background check on him. Why wouldn't they? It was pretty much standard procedure.

But somehow, he hadn't expected Kramer to drop the bomb like that, especially in front of Katy.

He told himself it didn't matter, since there wasn't anything more than friendship between them. But that argument would have gone further if they hadn't just shared a bone-rattling kiss.

A kiss he'd desperately wanted to repeat.

His intent had been just to offer comfort, but suddenly he'd kissed her, and even more incredibly, she'd kissed him back. He'd wanted the kiss to go on forever, but he knew that it was probably one-sided. No doubt her response had been in reaction to surviving a horrible experience rather than any true feelings toward him.

Duke nudged his hand with his nose, as if sensing his inner turmoil, and he bent down to scratch the silky spot between the dog's ears, grateful for his silent companion. After the way Deputy Kramer had reacted back there, he wished he'd sent Duke after the blond guy to prove he actually existed. But he'd been too worried about Katy to think clearly.

Not that he had regrets over his split-second decision. Katy's life was more important than his reputation, any day.

He squared his shoulders and told himself he didn't care what Deputy Kramer thought about him. He knew the blond dude existed, and given enough time, he'd find a way to prove it.

As he approached the motel, Duke growled low in his throat. Reese slowed his pace, peering through the darkness.

"What is it, boy?" he whispered. Duke was too well trained to growl for no reason, so he pulled out his weapon, the spare one he'd grabbed from his house when Katy had driven him there, and slid a bullet into the chamber.

The half-moon in the sky offered some light, and a quick glance at his watch verified dawn would be breaking soon. The area around the motel was deserted for once, and he wasn't sure if that was a good thing or not. He edged closer to the brick wall of the motel, trying to stay out of sight while looking for anything out of place.

When he approached the door to the motel room, Duke seemed to tense up, as if ready to spring. Glancing down, Reese could see the broken doorknob.

He considered calling Deputy Kramer but decided it would take too long for the guy to get here, and really, if the blond dude was inside, he wanted to be the one to take him down.

Lifting his foot, he kicked open the door at the same time he commanded the dog, "Attack."

Duke didn't waste a second, leaping over the threshold the way he'd been trained to do.

Reese peered around the edge of the door, his weapon ready, but there was no one inside. He knew for sure the place was empty by the way Duke sniffed along the floor, going into the bathroom and then coming back out again. The dog came right up to where he stood, looking up at him expectantly.

A stab of disappointment slashed deep. He went into the room, looking for anything out of place. Why would the blond guy come here after being at Katy's? What had he been looking for?

Then he remembered the cardboard box that held all his notes and photos of boot prints that he'd taken while investigating the poaching activity.

With a sick feeling in his stomach, he disengaged his weapon and set it aside so he could begin to search the room, trying to remember where he'd left the box. The motel room wasn't very large, and it didn't take long for him to realize it was gone.

The blond dude had stolen it.

Reese sat down hard on the edge of the bed, scrubbing his hands over his face. Granted, the police had evidence, too, but this was his case, and that box had contained his evidence.

He let out a heavy sigh and pulled out his phone to dial the sheriff's department. No matter what they thought, he needed to follow the book and file a police report.

But deep down, Reese knew that Deputy Kramer would only assume this was all part of his master plan. He imagined the deputy would even accuse him of breaking his own motel room door to make it look as if he'd been robbed.

He was the only one who knew the truth. What was that old saying? The truth shall set you free?

Yeah, not so much. Reese had a bad feeling the truth wasn't going to be enough to keep him out of jail.

But what hurt the most would be the stark disappointment in Katy's eyes when she believed what the deputy was saying.

8

Katy picked through the mess left in her living room, trying to figure out what, if anything, was salvageable, inwardly reeling from Deputy Kramer's revelation.

Reese was in debt. So much so that the police didn't believe his story about the poacher working with a blond guy.

She didn't want to believe Reese was involved. But he hadn't denied the allegations; in fact, he'd looked guilty. As if the deputy had revealed a secret. And really, why would Ian make something like that up?

Very simply, he wouldn't.

The deputy was still in her kitchen, making notes about the crime scene. She replaced a drawer from one of her end tables, thinking she should probably offer to make a pot of coffee.

Why not? The caffeine wouldn't be the only thing keeping her awake.

She headed into the kitchen in time to hear Ian speaking into his radio.

"He's saying someone broke into his motel room?" Deputy Kramer asked incredulously. "Come on, you've got to be kidding me."

Katy froze in the act of reaching for her canister of coffee. The deputy had to be talking about Reese.

"Yeah, fine. I'll head over there, but I'm sure this is nothing more than a ruse to deflect his guilt."

Katy stared blindly down at the counter. Was it possible she'd been wrong about Reese?

Thinking back, she remembered the grim expression in Reese's eyes when they'd come upon his smashed truck. The stark fear he'd shown when they'd been nearly run off the road by the black vehicle barreling down on them.

The concern in his eyes when he'd told her that Boyle needed her medical expertise more than he did.

"I'm sorry, Dr. Katy, but I need to head over to the motel," Deputy Kramer said with obvious regret. "Make sure you lock up the door behind me."

She looked up and caught his gaze. "I'm coming with you."

His eyes widened in dismay. "I don't think that's a good idea. Better for you to keep your distance from that guy. As far as I'm concerned, he's nothing but trouble."

"I'm coming," she repeated, her mind made up. "You can't stop me from going over to the motel."

"No, but I can stop you from getting anywhere near the crime scene," he said grimly. "Even better, I could have you arrested for interfering with a police investigation."

His threat was nothing but a bluff, and she knew it. He'd never get away with arresting one of the ER doctors for something so ridiculous; he'd never live it down. For one thing, she'd helped a lot of people in this town, earning their respect. Not to mention that her absence would leave the hospital short staffed in the height of tourist season.

The news would spread through the community faster than the gossip that she and Reese had shared a meal at Rose's Café.

Ian turned to leave, which was fine with her. She went into her bedroom to throw on a sweatshirt, jeans and sneakers. After pulling her long hair into a simple ponytail, she grabbed her purse and walked out to her car. Granted, the motel was close enough to walk, but it was the middle of the night, and being awoken from a sound sleep by an intruder made her feel a bit skittish.

Foolish of her to take the car, she soon realized, since the sheriff's deputies had blocked the motel parking lot with their vehicles. She pulled into the parking lot of the Gas N' Go station located right across the street. The night air was chilly despite being June, so she was glad she had on her sweatshirt as she walked over to the motel.

Despite his threat, Deputy Kramer ignored her when she walked up. "So you say the only thing missing is a shoe box full of photos and notes about the poachers," Deputy Kramer said with a hint of sarcasm in his tone.

She tried to catch Reese's gaze, but he seemed to be avoiding her. Duke stood patiently at his side, and she was struck by the knowledge that the dog really would risk his life to protect Reese.

"Yes, that's correct," Reese said in a low tone. The resigned expression on his face indicated that he knew Deputy Kramer didn't believe him.

"But not your notebook computer," the deputy pressed. "Why wouldn't the poacher take that, too? Why just the box? Surely he'd assume you had notes on the computer, as well."

"I don't know," Reese said mildly. "But I'll be sure to ask him if I see him."

Deputy Kramer scowled. "This isn't a joke, Webster. Filing false police reports could land you in the slammer."

"It's not a false report," Reese said. "I know you don't believe me, but I needed to get this on record, in case anything happens to me later."

Katy couldn't help feeling sick to her stomach at the thought of anything happening to Reese. Even worse, it seemed Reese believed it was only a matter of time till the blond guy caught up to him.

"I suppose you believe the guy went to Dr. Katy's house first, to look for the box, and then came here," Deputy Kramer scoffed.

Reese lifted a brow. "Why not? The timing worked out perfectly."

"Is there anyone who can vouch for the fact that this shoe box of evidence even existed?"

Reese glanced at her briefly but then looked away without saying anything.

She thought back to the night she'd taken him to his house deep in the woods after finding his smashed truck. He'd come out of the house carrying a computer case, his duffel bag and, she remembered now, a shoe box.

"I can," she said. "I can vouch for the fact that Reese had a shoe box with him."

Ian stared at her, his expression full of skeptic disbelief.

"You don't have to do this," Reese said in a low tone.

She smiled sadly. "Yes, I do." She turned toward Deputy Kramer with firm resolve. "I gave Mr. Webster a ride out to his truck the night he was shot. We came around the curve, saw that his truck had been smashed to pieces, so I drove him to his house so he could pick up his dog and some things to take with him to the motel. When he came out of the house, he had a duffel bag, a computer case and a small, square box."

Kramer didn't write anything down in his notebook, tucking it away instead.

"Okay, I'll file the report," he said curtly. He turned away to join the other deputy, who was walking around the area, for what purpose, she had no idea.

"I'm sorry I dragged you into this," Reese said, his expression grim. "But hopefully you're safe now that the poacher has what he was looking for."

She nodded, trying to think of something to say. "But he could still come after you," she pointed out.

"Duke and I can handle it if he does, right boy?" Reese bent over to run his hand over Duke's sleek fur. Well, it looked soft, but that was only a guess since she'd never touched the animal. "Hank promised to have the rental car here by noon, so I'll be able to head home. Besides, you'll be safer if you stay far away from me."

The finality of his tone hit hard. She wanted to protest, to tell him that she was willing to take the risk, but she didn't.

Because he was right. She sensed she would be safer with some distance between them. Although, honestly, that wasn't the real problem. The issue was that they were complete opposites for anything more than friendship.

No matter how much she longed to be held in his arms. To share another kiss.

She swallowed hard. "Take care, Reese," she murmured before turning away.

"Wait, I'll walk you home."

"No need," she said, her tone sharper than she intended. "My car is right across the street."

She continued across the street to where she'd left her car. It was only when she slid behind the wheel that she caught one last glimpse of Reese standing there with Duke at his side.

Blinking back ridiculous tears, she drove home.

REESE WANTED nothing more than to chase after Katy, but he forced himself to stay where he was.

He hadn't been lying. Katy would be much safer if she stayed far away from him. And keeping her safe had to be the top priority.

Besides, he knew full well how horrified Katy had been to hear how far he was in debt. Granted, he was making steady progress, but he still wasn't debt free. Katy didn't realize that he'd never take any of her money to free himself from his financial burden. Call it pride, or pig-headed stubbornness, but there was no way he'd accept money from a woman.

Especially not someone he cared about.

Suzanne's mess was his problem alone. Plenty of people had told him to hire a lawyer to go after her, forcing the issue that she should share in the debt since she'd created ninety percent of it, but he'd refused.

The taillights from Katy's car disappeared from view, and he steeled his resolve by turning back toward the motel. Duke trotted off to water a bush, so he waited before heading inside his motel room. The door was still broken, but he wasn't worried. He had Duke and firmly believed that the blond dude was long gone.

Falling asleep wasn't easy; he tossed and turned to the point that Duke padded over, sticking his nose against Reese's chest as if to ask *what's wrong?*

He buried his face against the dog's neck for a moment, wishing things could be different. But wallowing in self-pity was one thing he'd promised himself he wouldn't do, so he lifted his head and gave Duke a nice rub. "Good boy. Lie down, Duke. Down."

Duke dropped down and stretched out on his belly. Reese flopped back on the bed, staring at the ceiling, knowing he should be grateful for what he had. Although at times like this, when everything seemed stacked against him, it wasn't easy.

Somehow, he found himself reaching for faith and God.

Please keep Katy safe and provide me the strength and courage I'll need as I search for the man responsible for all of this. Amen.

He must have slept, because Duke's low growl, combined with bright sunlight, brought him instantly awake.

"What is it, boy?" he asked, blinking the remnants of sleep from his eyes.

Duke stayed right in front of the door, the hair on the scruff of his neck standing upright. Reese dragged on his cargo shorts, T-shirt and running shoes, checking his weapon as he walked over to where Duke waited. He tucked his gun into his holster and grabbed a water bottle.

He found himself hoping the blond dude had returned to finish what he'd started. Getting him in custody would salvage Reese's reputation.

He pulled open the door, and Duke ran through the opening and immediately crossed the parking lot. Reese had little choice but to sprint after him.

"Duke, halt!" he called sharply when several bystanders shied away in fear.

Duke stopped on a dime and turned his head to look

back at Reese. The dog's muscles were quivering, and Reese knew that something was up.

"Search, Duke," he commanded.

The dog sprinted forward again, and this time, Reese ran to keep up with him as he crossed the road and headed in the direction of the hiking trail.

Had the blond dude come this way? If so, Reese was certain that, with Duke's help, he'd find him, proving that he existed once and for all.

WITH HER DAY off stretching long and empty before her, Katy finished cleaning up the mess in her home and then tried to think of something to do.

Something that didn't involve going back to the motel to find Reese. The weather report predicted another steamy day with temperatures reaching ninety degrees or more, and the interior of her house was already too warm and stifling. Opening up the windows helped a little as there was a bit of a breeze coming off the lake.

She couldn't bear the thought of being around other people, her emotions from the night before leaving her raw and vulnerable. She had a few options; stay cooped up in her steamy house on a sunny day, offer to work for one of her colleagues, or take a walk on the hiking trail.

If she called one of her colleagues, offering to work, she'd have to field a bunch of questions about what was going on, so in the end, the hiking trail won. Especially because she needed a distraction from the fact Reese would be leaving town today to head back home.

She changed into a pair of shorts, a loose gauzy shirt, and a tank top. The hiking trail was used by many of the citizens of Crystal Lake, herself included, but that was before she knew about the cougars and bears. Running into wildlife wasn't her idea of fun and was almost enough to keep her home.

But her colleague, Gabe Allen, often ran the trails, and he'd never seen any real wildlife other than the occasional white-tailed deer. And he often told the story about how he'd met his wife, Larissa, on the trail, coming to her rescue when she'd hurt her ankle.

There was nothing to be afraid of, right? Right.

Squaring her shoulders, she lathered up with sunscreen since her fair skin tended to burn and freckle, grabbed a water bottle and headed outside. The hour was early enough that the sun wasn't too brutal yet, and hopefully, she'd be home by lunchtime.

The trail wasn't too far from her house, located in the opposite direction of town, so she decided to walk. No sense in driving to the hiking trail, she thought with a wry grin.

Lifting her face to the sun, she marveled at the warmth seeping into her pores. The scent of burning wood filled the air, reminding her of the campfire they'd had during the one summer she attended Girl Scout camp. A venture that hadn't lasted long. She'd screamed like a banshee when one of her bunkmates had put a grass snake in her bed.

Maybe a grass snake was totally harmless, but she hadn't cared. She'd never gone back to Girl Scout camp after that one disastrous experience. She'd spent her next few summers at the library, reading every book she could get her hands on and enjoying every moment of peace and quiet.

Her camp counselor would laugh herself silly to know that Katy was now living rural Wisconsin, braving a hike along the trail all by herself.

The trail wound around with a steadily rising terrain. The locals called it a hill, but in her opinion it was more like a small mountain, especially surrounded by woods the way it was. She was surprised that the scent of burning wood grew stronger rather than dissipating at the higher elevation.

Where was that campfire anyway? Was someone camping out toward the top of the hill? The idea was enough to make her think about turning around to go back home.

Maybe she should go back to the motel to find Reese? The DNR would be interested in someone camping illegally, wouldn't it? Especially since there was a campground located a few miles down the highway.

She was so lost in her thoughts that she wasn't paying attention to where she was walking. Her left foot stepped in a hole, and she cried out as her ankle twisted in pain.

After hobbling over to a rock, she looked down at her ankle. It wasn't as bad as she'd feared, so she took off the gauze shirt she'd tied around her waist and tried to rip off the sleeves. But the material was strong, and she had to look around for something to use.

She found a sharp-edged rock and used that to rend the fabric. The sleeve came off easily with the rock's help, and she pulled off the other sleeve, too, so that it would match. She wound the fabric around her ankle for support and then took a long gulp from her water bottle.

So much for her hike, she thought grimly. Now, for sure, she'd have to head back down. Which was probably best, since she wasn't too keen on meeting up with the illegal campers. The scent that had started out so nice was almost unbearably strong now. In fact, there was a haze hovering in the air, making her eyes water.

She rose to her feet, swiping at her burning eyes with the remnants of the second sleeve of her gauze shirt. She blinked again, realizing that she could barely see a few feet in front of her face.

What in the world was going on? She couldn't see more than a yard or two of the trail.

She turned in a small circle, trying to get her bearings. She knew she needed to go down rather than head farther up the trail and took a few steps in order to get a sense of which direction she should head.

The downward slope beneath her feet helped provide direction as the smoke was becoming unbearable. Tears pricked at her eyes, and smoke clogged her throat, making her cough.

Half blind, she stumbled down the trail, hoping and praying she was going in the right direction.

But she abruptly froze in horror when she heard a low, menacing growl.

9

Reese desperately searched for a cell signal on his phone, knowing he needed to get help, and fast. Duke had led him farther up the trail toward the scent of a campfire. But the smoke was getting thicker and thicker, making him fear the worst.

What might have begun as a small campfire started by kids or careless adults had somehow gotten out of control into something very dangerous. After almost five weeks of no rain, the level of fire danger in this area was pretty high.

He climbed up on a boulder, holding his phone up, trying to see if there was a signal. Was there one bar there? Hope swelled as he pushed the button to make a call, but after several long moments, there was nothing.

Lost signal.

Sliding off the rock, he continued taking the trail. Duke's growl had him slowing to a stop, every sense on alert. Was the blond guy nearby?

"What is it, boy?" he asked in a low tone.

In answer, Duke let out a sharp bark. But the dog's wagging tail was reassuring. Reese trusted Duke's senses better than his own, especially at times like this. Duke bounded down the trail, disappearing in a haze of smoke.

Reese scrambled to keep up with his dog, wondering what had caught Duke's attention. Right now, all he wanted to do was to call his boss to report the possible fire, but he couldn't do that without a cell signal.

"Help me!" a female voice cried.

"Duke, down," he instinctively shouted, putting on speed. The smoke was so thick he almost trampled over Katy, who was sprawled on the ground staring up at Duke with fear blazing from her eyes. "Good boy," he said when he realized that Duke was actually protecting Katy.

"Good boy?" she wheezed, cringing from the dog. "He scared me to death!"

"I'm sorry about that, but you know he's well trained. He truly was trying to protect you," Reese said mildly. "You can tell by the way he was standing guard. Here, take my hand," he instructed.

She grasped his hand, winced and then coughed as she rose to her feet. He was surprised to see her here, especially after everything that had happened the night before, or rather, just a few hours ago. She tugged on her hand, and he reluctantly released her. She winced again when taking a step back, and he dropped his gaze, searching for the cause of her discomfort. Based on the makeshift bandage around her ankle, he suspected a twist or a sprain.

"What happened?" he asked with a frown.

"It's fine," she said in a hoarse tone. "But we need to get away from here. The smoke is getting worse."

"I know. It's bad up here," he agreed. But he couldn't leave just yet. "Duke will lead you down the trail," he assured her. "I need to investigate that fire, in case there are people stranded up there."

"No, there's nothing you can do," she protested. The frank fear in her gaze and the way she lightly grasped his arm tugged at his heart. The way she looked at him now, it was as if the nightmare from last night hadn't happened. "The faster we get down the trail, the better chance we have of getting help. Surely someone in town has noticed the smoke. Help must be on the way."

True, he'd thought the same thing. Surely the sheriff's deputies had noticed the smoke from the campfire by now. But he couldn't force himself to leave the scene of what just might be another crime.

He'd thought at first that Duke had left the motel because he'd been on the blond guy's trail, but now he knew that it was the smoke that had captured the dog's attention. Maybe the fire was the result of careless kids, but it was also possible the fire had been started on purpose, although he didn't want to tell Katy that. She'd been frightened enough already.

"Duke will show you the way back. I'll join you as soon as I can. I just need to be sure there isn't anyone else trapped up here."

Katy's terrified expression turned grim at the thought of other potential victims, and he was impressed by the way she pulled herself together. "All right, but please hurry," she murmured. "I don't like the idea of you risking your life."

She didn't seem to understand that risking his life was his responsibility. He might be a DNR game warden rather than a cop, but he had much the same kind of training. There could be campers up there in danger, and he wasn't about to leave without checking things out. "I will." He turned to the German shepherd, giving him a signal with his hand. "Home, Duke. Lead Katy home."

Duke seemed to understand, taking a few steps down

the path and then glancing back as if to make sure Katy was following.

Katy looked as if she wanted to argue but reluctantly turned and hobbled toward Duke. He wanted to haul her close and kiss her again but made himself turn and head up the trail instead. The smoke grew thicker the higher he went. The wind shifted, and he sucked in a harsh breath when he saw the orange flames dancing along the tops of the trees.

This was way more than a campfire gone out of control. This was a full-fledged wildfire.

Looking at the blaze, he couldn't help thinking there was no way this was truly the result of careless kids.

Something deep in his gut told him there was a good chance the fire had been started on purpose.

KATY SWIPED at her tearing eyes and stumbled after Duke, trying to follow his bobbing tail. Her initial fear of the dog faded when, on the few occasions she lost sight of him, he doubled back, returning to her side and nudging her gently, as if herding a lost lamb.

She didn't like leaving Reese behind, and she sensed Duke didn't like it much, either. Maybe the smoke was wreaking havoc with her brain cells, but she got the feeling that Duke was trying to rush her down the trail so that he could get back to his owner.

Truthfully, she couldn't blame him.

The toe of her running shoe caught a root, and she stumbled, managing to catch herself before face-planting in the dirt. Duke materialized by her side, nudging her with his head.

"Good boy," she murmured, rubbing the silky fur behind

his ears. She wasn't sure how it had happened, but in the last fifteen minutes, he'd gone from scaring the daylights out of her to being her best friend. She could easily understand now why Reese was so attached to him. And why German shepherds made great police dogs.

The air was slightly clearer down near the ground, and it occurred to her that lack of oxygen was a serious threat. She couldn't deny the fact that smoke filling her lungs might have caused her to stumble in the first place. Carbon monoxide poisoning was no joke, and if she didn't do something, she might not make it off the trail even with Duke leading the way.

Thinking fast, she pulled what was left of her gauze shirt off her waist, dampened it with her water bottle and then tied it over her nose and mouth. Almost instantly, her breathing was easier, without the constant feeling of having shards of glass stuck in her throat, although she sensed the damp fabric wouldn't filter the air for long.

Hopefully long enough to get off this stupid hiking trail.

Duke nudged her again and made a high-pitched whining sound as if urging her to hurry. She rose to her feet and continued following him, trusting in the dog's sense of direction more than her own. In the distance, she could hear sirens and hoped that meant fire trucks were on the way. Maybe once the firefighters arrived, Reese wouldn't feel the need to search for the campers who'd started the fire, handing off the investigation to the professionals instead.

Duke let out several loud barks, startling her badly. Her steps faltered to a stop, as she sensed his barking wasn't a good sign.

The dog appeared at her side, circled around her and then let out three more short barks. The animal was clearly trying to tell her something, but what? He turned and went off the trail, heading south. When she didn't immediately follow, he came back, did that strange whinny sound in his throat and went off the trail again, looking back at her as if to yell, *follow me!*

What should she do? Why would the dog lead her off the trail? She sensed if Reese were here, he'd tell her to trust the dog. Without a second thought, she climbed up and over a boulder, slipping and sliding on the rocky terrain, her ankle throbbing in earnest without the firmness of the trail. It wasn't until she climbed yet another boulder that she could see the flames licking the treetops. And not just the trees behind her but in every direction she could see.

Her heart nearly stopped in her chest as the horror of what she was seeing seeped into her brain.

She and Duke were literally surrounded by fire.

REESE PULLED OFF HIS T-SHIRT, doused it with water and pulled it up over his nose and mouth. Too bad he didn't have eye protection, as he could barely see through the smoke.

He turned around and headed back down the path in the direction of where he'd left Katy and Duke. Rescuing campers was one thing, but seeing the flames of the fire engulfing the tops of the trees put everything in a new perspective. The entire town was at risk if this fire spread farther. And he wasn't sure there even were campers to rescue.

Reese went as fast as he dared, barely able to see through the thick smoke. He was a little surprised he hadn't stumbled across any other hikers aside from Katy. Surely they hadn't been the only ones on the trail, although it was possible the steamy hot temperatures had deterred some of the tourists. Boating, skiing, and fishing on Crystal Lake were the main attractions during the summer months, not the hiking trails.

Reese didn't call out for Duke, hoping that his dog had already gotten Katy off the trail and down to safety. He could hear the wail of sirens indicating that help was coming. But the Hope County Fire Department was far too small to take on a forest fire. Normal protocol was to call the DNR as well as every fire department within a fifty-mile radius. He hoped every single one of them was already on its way.

As he fought his way through the smoke, back down the trail, Reese remembered how calm and peaceful he'd felt after praying. Was God listening to Katy's prayers right now? He wanted to believe that was the case and found himself adding his own prayer.

Please save us, Lord! Save us from the fire!

Three short barks reached his ears, and he paused on the trail, breathing hard through the damp fabric of his shirt. Three short barks from Duke indicated danger, and the realization that Katy and Duke weren't safe at all spurred him into action.

Despite the thick smoke, he slipped and slid down the path in the direction from where he thought the barks had come. Although being surrounded by smoke was disorienting, so he couldn't be sure he was headed the right way.

Sweat, or maybe it was smoke, burned his eyes. "Duke?" he croaked, just in case the dog and Katy were nearby. "Come, Duke!"

There was an answering bark, and he smiled grimly behind the shirt. He couldn't understand why they were still on the hill, unless Katy had fallen again, injuring her ankle to the point she couldn't walk. And if that was the case, he knew Duke wouldn't leave her alone.

Even if it meant succumbing to smoke inhalation poisoning right alongside her.

Despite the overwhelming heat, smoke and sweat, a chill snaked its way down his spine. He couldn't bear the thought of losing either of them, so he shoved the negative thoughts aside and concentrated on following the sounds of Duke's barking.

It seemed like hours but was probably only ten minutes or so before Duke burst out through the smoke to greet him. He dropped to his knees and hugged the animal gratefully.

"Good boy," he murmured. "Good boy!"

The dog wiggled away and barked. He understood the animal was trying to tell him something, so he slowly stood. "Find Katy," he said.

Duke headed off the path, and Reese followed, snaking around rocks and boulders. He trusted Duke, even though he couldn't figure out why the animal wasn't leading them out of the fire.

He slipped and landed hard on a rock but quickly forced himself upright. "Katy?" he called, forcing air through his sore throat. "Are you all right?"

"I'm here." Her reply was so faint he almost thought he'd imagined it. She must be injured, or he was certain she would have come to meet him.

"Hang on, okay? I'll be there soon."

Following Duke off the trail wasn't nearly as easy, as the animal slipped under a fallen tree branch that Reese had to crawl over. He was glad they were still heading downward, if not on the path.

Maybe it was his imagination, but he thought the smoke was thinner as he followed Duke's winding path. At least his eyes weren't burning as much.

"Reese! Over here," Katy called. He caught a glimpse of

her red hair and felt the tightness ease in his chest when he realized she was sitting under a tree about twenty yards up ahead. He was amazed that she'd tied fabric over her face, the same way he had, to protect her airway as much as possible. Most hikers wouldn't think of that, but then again, she was a doctor.

"What happened?" he asked as he made his way closer. "Did you fall and hurt your ankle again?"

"No, Duke led me this way," she said in a stronger voice. "He was pretty insistent about it, too."

"Good boy, Duke," he said, praising the dog again for saving their lives. "We're still heading down, which is good, but I'm not sure I understand why he led you off the trail."

Katy slowly rose to her feet as he came closer. "I'm so glad you're here," she said in a low tone. "I'm not as afraid."

He reached out and pulled her gently into his arms. He was dirty, sweaty and smelly, but he couldn't resist holding her at least for a moment.

She hugged him back, and despite the seriousness of their situation, he found himself smiling.

"How are we going to get out of here?" she asked, her voice muffled against his shirt.

Regretfully, he loosened his grip enough to look down at her. They both looked like bandits from the Old West with their noses and mouths covered, but he figured this wasn't the time to point that out.

"We're going to be fine," he assured her with all the confidence he could muster. "Duke will get us out of trouble, won't you, boy?"

Duke lifted his head, his ears perking up when he heard his name. He wagged his tail and then turned to continue on a convoluted path that only he could see.

"Can you walk?" he asked Katy.

"Yes, but I don't know that it's going to help much," she said as she followed him down the rocky path.

"Why not? Surely you're not still afraid of Duke after all this?"

"No, not at all. He's a wonderful guard dog, and I'm sure I'd already be dead if not for him guiding me." Katy was silent for a few minutes as they carefully picked their way over the boulders and fallen tree branches littering the side of the hill. "Duke pushed me off the trail and I think it's because there's more fire down there."

He snapped his head up and looked over at her. "I didn't see any sign of fire from my vantage point up above."

Katy's gaze was full of despair. "Trust me, I saw it. I just don't see how we're going to get out of this mess."

"We'll find a way," he assured her, even though his mind was reeling at the news. If the fire was truly surrounding them, they were definitely in trouble. But how could the fire have gotten over to the southeast when the wind was coming from that direction? The fire should be heading away from them, which was one of the reasons that he'd sent Duke with Katy to keep her safe.

"It doesn't make sense," he muttered. "There shouldn't be any fire coming from that way, not unless someone set it on purpose."

"Maybe someone did set it on purpose," Katy said. "Because I know that I saw fire. Duke saw it, too, which is why he led me off the trail."

The implication sank deep. Reese knew with sick certainty that this was the work of the blond guy. The same guy who'd tried to kill them on the freeway.

The same guy who'd broken into Katy's house and his motel room.

Was this his final goal? To get rid of him and Katy once and for all?

Okay, he needed to get a grip. Who'd started the fire and why were the least of their concerns. They needed to find a way to get to safety. Duke was still following some sort of trail, and Reese tried to remain positive, although it wasn't easy.

Katy was saying something softly under her breath, and he soon realized that she was reciting the Lord's Prayer. The verse echoed in his mind, drudged up from a distant memory from the last time he'd attended church, before Suzanne had left him for his best friend.

He found himself saying the prayer with Katy as they followed Duke.

And when the prayer was over, a strange sense of peace surrounded him.

"Oomph," Katy said as she slipped and fell on her backside.

"Are you all right?" he asked, reaching out for her at the same time he was trying not to do the same thing.

"I'm fine, but do you hear that?" she asked, her eyes lighting up with hope.

For a moment, he wondered if she'd hit her head, or maybe the smoke had gotten to her. "Hear what?"

"That noise." She hastily scrambled to her feet, looking around in earnest. "It sounds like water."

"Water?" He searched the rocky landscape for Duke and found the dog several yards down near a cluster of boulders. When the dog lifted his head, Reese thought for sure he saw water dripping from the animal's muzzle.

"There is water, see?" Katy said excitedly. "Duke found it! Good boy, Duke! Good boy!"

He followed Katy down to where Duke waited near the

water. As much as he knew water was vital to their survival, he couldn't bear to burst her bubble.

Because even with water to wet their clothes and hydrate their bodies, he knew they were far from safe.

If the fire truly surrounded them on all sides, he didn't know how on earth they'd make it out of here alive.

10

Katy pulled the gauze shirt off her face and cupped her hands in the stream, drinking greedily even though she didn't know if the water was safe for consumption.

At this moment, a parasite of some sort was the least of their concerns. Besides, the way Duke had lapped up the water was good enough for her.

The dog stayed by her side, even when Reese joined them at the stream. When she finished drinking, she leaned over and wrapped her arms around the animal's neck, giving Duke a big hug.

"You're an awesome dog, you know that?" she whispered against his damp fur. "I don't know what we would have done without you."

"I agree," Reese said after he'd finished drinking from the stream. He sat back on his heels and looked at her. A smile kicked up the corner of his mouth. "I'm glad to see you're not afraid of him anymore."

She lifted her head, surprisingly reluctant to let the dog go. "I feel stupid for being afraid of him in the first place," she admitted. "He's amazing. I understand now why people get so attached to their pets."

"Not stupid," Reese corrected swiftly. "He's trained to attack, so being cautious around him was smart. But he'd never hurt you. In fact, he'd protect you with his life."

"Me?" She frowned and shook her head. "No, he'd protect you before me."

"Not if I told him to protect *you*."

The intense expression in Reese's eyes made her shiver, despite the heat and smoke. Was Reese really willing to put his life on the line for her? His dog's life on the line for her? No one had ever done something like that for her before, but then again, she'd never been in this kind of danger before, either.

Thinking back to the way Deputy Kramer had treated Reese, she couldn't suppress a flash of anger. No way in the world would she believe Reese was the poacher, and he didn't deserve the wild accusations the deputy had thrown at him. So what if he was in debt? Half of America was in debt! That didn't mean anything.

Reese had always treated her like a gentleman, and heaven help her, she was beginning to care about him, far more than she should. He was strong, kind and gentle, all at the same time. If things were different...

But they weren't. Besides, this wasn't the time or place for a heart-to-heart, soul-baring discussion. They needed to find a way to get off this stupid hill to safety.

"Do you think Duke can find a way out of here?" she asked, changing the subject. "He's been amazing so far."

"Maybe." Reese bent over the stream, filling his water bottle as much as possible. "Hand me yours, too."

She was surprised she'd managed to hang on to her empty container, especially after following Duke over the rocky terrain. The bottle was badly crumpled, but that didn't matter since Reese could only fill it halfway.

"Now we need to get our clothes wet," he instructed her. "I'll go first and then back off to give you some privacy."

She nodded, understanding his reasoning. Their clothes wouldn't stay wet for long, but since they were surrounded by fire, they needed every possible advantage they could get.

"Maybe we should follow the water," she suggested, averting her gaze, too, as Reese lay down in the stream, face down and then rolling onto his back. He shouldn't be getting his stitches wet, but she decided not to say anything since they were both covered with soot and grime, anyway. If his wound was going to get infected, it didn't much matter what the source was.

She might have laughed at how he looked, like a giant fish flapping around in the shallow water, if their situation weren't so grim.

"Your turn," he said, rivets of water running off him as he climbed back up on the rocks.

Normally she would have felt self-conscious about rolling around in the stream, but the cool water felt so good she couldn't bring herself to care. She had to force herself to get out when all she really wanted to do was to bask in the cool bliss.

Reese had his back turned to her as promised, but she could tell he was searching the landscape around them, no doubt figuring out their next move. A realization that brought her back to their harsh reality.

"Ready?" he asked when she came up to stand beside him.

"Yes." Really, she had no choice but to be ready, but if he was going to maintain a positive attitude, so was she. "Is it my imagination or is there less smoke down here near the water?"

"Definitely less smoke," he said. "But I don't think we can afford to sit here and wait to be rescued. We need to keep moving. I'm hoping we'll run into the firefighters who'll be here fighting the blaze soon."

"That would be nice. Duke could find them, couldn't he?"

"I hope so." Reese shook out his wet T-shirt and pulled it on, drawing the collar up to cover his nose and mouth. She re-tied her freshly dampened gauze shirt over her lower face, too, knowing that they were likely going to see more smoke rather than less as they made their way out of here.

"Home, Duke. Take us home," Reese commanded.

The dog picked his way along the edge of the stream heading south. Their pace was slow since the uneven terrain was difficult even for the dog to navigate.

Her ankle didn't seem to hurt as much, but that could also be the result of an adrenaline rush from being in danger. She knew full well that basic survival instincts would always outweigh the mundane.

"Why haven't you asked me?" Reese said, his voice muffled by his cotton T-shirt.

"Ask you what?" They were walking single file, following Duke, so she couldn't get a good look at his eyes.

"If I'm guilty of poaching. Of planning all this to throw suspicion off me," he said.

"Deputy Kramer doesn't know what he's talking about, that's why. I was in the car with you when you saw your smashed truck, and the shock in your eyes was real. Plus, I was with you when that black truck came barreling down on us, nearly causing us to crash."

He didn't say anything in response, and she risked a

glance over her shoulder. His gaze met hers, and she saw the glint of hope reflected there. He wanted her to believe in him.

And she did.

"Do you remember that first night in the hospital?" she continued. "When I came over to take a look at your injury? You said, 'Marcus Boyle needs your medical expertise more than I do.' This was the guy you shot in self-defense, yet you were more worried about him than you were about yourself."

"I remember," he said. "I'm glad to hear you believe me, but I'm still surprised you haven't asked me any details about why I'm in debt."

She lifted a shoulder in a careless shrug, unwilling to admit she was, in fact, dying of curiosity to know the details. But Reese's personal life was none of her business. "I'm sure you have a good reason."

There was another long stretch of silence as they followed Duke's lead. When the dog crossed the stream, heading to the other side, Reese held out his hand to help her cross, too. Their fingers clung for a long, poignant moment before he released her.

"I was married once," Reese said, breaking the long silence. "While I was still in the navy. I heard the stories about cheating wives, women who were unable to handle the long separations, but I thought Suzanne and I were in love."

The hint of suffering in his tone made her want to hug him. "What happened?" she asked, even though she could guess.

"She proved me wrong. And then some."

"And then some?"

"Not only did she cheat on me, with my best friend, no

less, but she cleaned out our joint bank account and maxed out the credit card. When I came home from being at sea, the divorce papers were the only thing waiting for me. So I signed them and began to dig my way out of debt."

Her chest tightened with sorrow and anger. What he'd told her was so much worse than what she'd imagined. She glanced back at him again but tripped and stumbled. She would have fallen if not for Reese's quick reflexes. She clutched the muscles of his arms and stared up at him.

"I'm so sorry," she said. "What Suzanne did was unnecessarily cruel, and I can't imagine how you managed to get through it. I hope she had to pay at least half of that debt off."

She couldn't see his mouth covered by the T-shirt, but his eyes crinkled at the corners, which made her think he might be smiling. "No, I signed the papers, sold the house to pay off as much as I could and then went to a lawyer to consolidate what was left into monthly payments. I'd be in worse shape if my boss weren't allowing me to live in that log cabin for dirt cheap."

She put a hand on his arm, trying to think of something to say. But in truth, her mind was still reeling from what Reese had gone through. Most men would be angry and bitter and would have dragged their ex-wife through court to force the issue, but he hadn't. He'd taken on the responsibility without complaining.

He'd isolated himself from civilization, choosing to live in the woods with only his dog for company while dedicating his life to keeping the natural resources and wildlife safe.

Now that she knew the truth, it was easier to understand why he'd made the decisions he had.

Duke let out a sharp bark, interrupting the moment. She dropped her hand and turned away, heading after the dog.

They walked in silence for several moments. A coughing fit caught her off guard, forcing her to stop and bend over, bracing herself with her hands on her knees, to catch her breath.

When she stood, the swirling smoke burned her eyes. "It's worse," she croaked. "The smoke is getting worse."

"I know." Reese's grim tone surprised her after his previous determination to remain positive. The serious expression reflected in his eyes couldn't be denied.

She knew what he was trying to tell her. That it was possible that they might not make it out of here after all.

She closed her eyes for a moment and prayed.

Dear Lord, please give us the strength and courage we need to get out of here, and guide us to safety. Amen.

REESE WISHED MORE than anything he could reassure Katy that they would be fine, but he couldn't bear to lie to her. Not now. Not after she'd offered her unconditional trust. Something no one else had done for him, ever.

Maybe that's why he'd spilled his guts about Suzanne, when he hadn't told anyone else the full story, not even his boss.

No, the real reason he'd told Katy the truth was that he didn't want her to think the worst about him, like he was some sort of closet gambler or something. If he were honest, he'd admit that he cared about what Katy thought about him.

Ridiculous to even worry about that now, when they weren't anywhere close to being safe. What did it matter what she thought about him if they died?

No, they weren't going to die. He refused to believe they'd fail. Somehow, someway, they were going to find a way out of here.

Looking down, he noticed Katy's eyes were closed and knew she was praying. He reached out and took her hand.

"Let's pray together."

Her emerald-green eyes opened in shock, but she nodded, holding on to his hands tightly.

"Dear Lord, we have faith in your strength and goodness," Katy said.

"We seek your mercy and guidance to help us find safety," Reese added.

"If it be Thy will, amen."

"Amen," Reese echoed.

"Thank you," Katy said. "I know faith is new to you, but we have to trust in God's plan."

"All right," he agreed. It had never occurred to him before that Suzanne's leaving him for Will Fischer was all part of God's master plan. At the time, he'd been angry and hurt, burying himself in work. But now that he looked back, he knew for certain that if his wife hadn't left him and cleaned out their bank account, he wouldn't be here today.

And he wouldn't have met Katy.

Even in the midst of the desperate situation they were currently battling, he was glad he was here with her.

"We better keep going," she said. Even though they were both dirty, sweaty and smelled like smoke, he wanted nothing more than to kiss her.

Duke barked again, urging them on. "We're coming, boy," he called to the dog. He followed Katy with a renewed sense of peace and determination.

Between Duke's instincts and God's support, he firmly believed they'd find a way out of here.

"The force of the stream is dwindling," Katy said, a frown puckering her forehead. "It can't be good if we run out of water."

He'd noticed the water seemingly drying up too. "It doesn't mean we're headed in the wrong direction," he pointed out. "Could just be that the fire behind us is interfering with the water source."

"Maybe."

He could tell by her tone she wasn't convinced. "We agreed to have faith," he reminded her. "Duke wouldn't lead us into fire."

"True," Katy agreed. "You should have seen the way he kept barking and circling around me when we were still on the trail. It was as if he was trying to talk to me."

"Three barks means danger, which is his way of warning you not to go closer."

"Very effective." She slipped again but quickly regained her balance, with the help of his hand holding hers.

"Is your ankle okay?" he asked.

"As good as your arm, I'm sure," she said dryly.

"Let me know if you need to lean on me." He didn't want to think about how difficult it would be to carry her through the smoky haze, making his way across the rocks and tree branches littering the ground. He would if necessary, but he'd rather she lean on him before her ankle got to the point she couldn't walk on it.

Duke abruptly changed course, heading southwest, a direction that would take them even farther from the hiking trail. As much as he trusted the dog's instincts, he couldn't help a gnawing sense of worry.

"Good boy, Duke," Katy called encouragingly. Apparently her faith in Duke hadn't wavered. "Home. Take us home."

"I think you're going to have to get a dog of your own," he said. "You're going to miss Duke once we're out of this mess."

"I'd love one, but he'd have to be as well trained as Duke," she said. "Although my schedule isn't the greatest when it comes to owning pets."

"My schedule can be challenging, too, but trust me, having a pet is worth the effort."

"I never understood that, until today." Katy's comment ended on another coughing fit, and Reese put his hand on her back, alarmed at the fact that he could barely see more than two feet in front of his face.

He wanted to have faith, but it wasn't easy. Duke wouldn't lead them astray, but it was possible the smoke was interfering with the dog's ability to follow a scent.

"Reese?" Katy's hoarse voice worried him, although his wasn't much better.

"I'm here, Katy. Hang on to me, I'll help you."

"No, that's not what I mean. Don't you hear it?"

He paused, straining to listen. Maybe he was losing it, but he didn't hear anything. "No, what do you hear?"

"A roaring sound, like a fire that's out of control. What if we're heading into more danger?"

He didn't want to think that Duke would lead them farther into fire, but before he could respond, a loud bang pierced the air.

"Get down," he said hoarsely, tugging on Katy's hand.

Katy dropped down to the ground, and Duke rushed toward them, a low, growling noise rumbling in his throat.

"Was that a gunshot?" Katy whispered, her red-rimmed eyes wide with horror.

"I'm not sure," he admitted. "We need to find cover just in case."

"What about over by that fallen log over there?" she said, pointing to a spot near the edge of the dried-up stream.

"That's good. But keep your head down as much as possible," he urged. "You go first, and I'll follow behind you."

"Okay." She stayed bent over as she picked her way back over the rocky streambed. Duke stayed right beside her, while Reese covered her back.

He was thankful that they didn't hear any more gunfire as they moved toward the downed tree. Katy reached it first and sank to the ground. Duke stood beside her, and he had to smile when she said, "Sit, Duke."

Reese sank down beside her. "Down, Duke."

Normally, the dog always followed his commands, but this time, the dog simply stood there for a long minute, nose in the air, his ears twitching as he listened.

Then, abruptly, the dog took off, racing across the terrain like a wolf scenting food. Reese shouted, "Stay, Duke. Stay!" but his voice was little more than a hoarse croak and had no impact on the dog whatsoever.

Duke disappeared from sight, leaving them on their own.

11

Katy gasped and then coughed as she watched Duke disappear into the smoky haze. "Why is he leaving us?"

"I'm not sure. Could be the smoke is making him confused." Reese sounded upset, and she didn't blame him.

She had no idea how they'd get out of here without following Duke's lead. Especially after they'd heard that loud bang. She shivered despite the heat.

"Do you think that was really a gunshot?" she asked, voicing her fears out loud. "Maybe we were wrong and it just sounded like one."

"Maybe. Possibly a branch dropping from a tree or something like that," Reese agreed. "But I don't want to lead you into danger, either."

They were already smack dab in the middle of danger, but she understood what he meant. It was hard enough to battle the smoke from the fire; what could they do if someone was waiting for them in the woods with a gun? She strained to listen, hoping Duke didn't become the gunman's target.

But there was nothing but silence and smoke surrounding them.

Katy wasn't sure how long they huddled behind the downed tree branch—time held little meaning at this point —but there was no denying the smoke was only getting worse.

"I think we'd better keep going," Reese finally said. "We can't stay here forever."

"Which way?" She agreed with his decision to move on. What difference did it make if they died from smoke inhalation or from a bullet? A bullet might be a quicker death.

She shook off the morbid thoughts. They needed to stay positive.

And keep praying.

"The same direction Duke took," Reese said, slowly rising to his feet. He held out his hand to her, and she took it, silently praying they were making the right decision.

Reese didn't let go of her hand, and she found she was grateful for the human contact now that it was just the two of them making their way through the woods.

She found herself reciting the Lord's Prayer again under her breath as they made their way in the general direction the dog had taken. Soon, Reese joined her, their voices gaining strength, despite their hoarse throats.

She stopped praying when she couldn't hear herself anymore because of the roaring sound that seemed to swell in magnitude as they wove their way between trees and over rocks. Katy couldn't help wondering if they were heading straight into the fire rather than away from it.

She wished she knew why Duke had taken off like that. She never would have imagined the dog would totally abandon them.

"Wait a minute." Reese tugged at her hand, halting her progress. "Look at the smoke."

She blinked, her eyes tearing up from the constant assault from the smoky haze. "I know. It's been getting worse all along."

"Not that. It's getting lighter in color. It's not black but more gray."

She shook her head, not understanding. "What difference does that make?"

"When you douse a fire with water, the smoke gets lighter." Reese coughed again. "Come on, maybe this is the way to the firefighters."

She wanted to believe they were close to being rescued, but Reese's color-of-smoke theory seemed lame. Besides, she couldn't really tell much difference.

Woof! Woof!

"Is that Duke?" she asked, half afraid she'd imagined the sound. If three barks meant danger, what did two mean?

"I think so, come on." Reese changed direction, as if trying to aim for the spot where the barking had come from. She followed him blindly, still hanging on to his hand as if it were a lifeline.

A few minutes later, Duke came running out from the trees, heading straight toward them.

Reese crouched low, giving the dog a huge hug. She reached down to pet Duke's fur, overwhelmed with relief.

"He's back," Katy murmured. "Good boy!"

"Look, he's brought the firefighters with him," Reese pointed out.

Sure enough, several firefighters, covered head to toe in black and yellow gear, emerged from the woods directly in front of them. The firefighters picked up their pace, rushing over to meet them.

Her knees buckled as realization dawned.

They were safe! God and Duke had saved them!

KATY DIDN'T REMEMBER much of the trip back out of the woods beyond the worst of the fire. Soon she and Reese were placed on side-by-side stretchers, wearing identical oxygen masks. She recognized Sam Torretti, the paramedic who was also the son of Sheriff Luke Torretti, when he bent over her.

"I don't like how red your lips are," he muttered.

"I'm sure we don't have carbon monoxide poisoning," she assured him.

"But you do have a headache, right?" Sam persisted.

She slowly nodded. The headache had only just started after they'd heard the loud noise they'd mistaken for a gunshot.

"Then I hate to tell you, but you might be worse off than you realize, Doc," Sam said in a dry tone. "We're taking you to Hope County Hospital first. From there, you may be transferred to Madison if you need hyperbaric treatments."

She didn't like being on the patient side of the stretcher, and she especially didn't like being told what kind of medical procedures she needed. She knew very well how to treat smoke inhalation.

"Hyperbaric treatments are only for severe cases," she protested. "We're not that bad off."

"I think I'll let another doctor make that decision," Sam said with a stern look. "You're my patient now."

"I'm not going to the hospital," Reese spoke up. "I need to take care of my dog. Can you give me a ride to the veterinary clinic?"

Sam glanced over with a frown. "Your boyfriend needs to go in for treatment, just like you do."

She was about to point out that Reese wasn't her boyfriend, but why bother? The whole town probably knew they'd spent time together. And soon, they'd hear about how they'd been rescued together too. "He's right about the dog needing care. Duke saved our lives." After everything they'd been through with Duke, no way was she leaving the dog behind. "Surely there's some sort of treatment you can do for him."

"Here, we can use a face tent to provide some oxygen," the other paramedic spoke up.

"Try it," Reese urged.

Duke didn't like the mask hanging around his neck, but at least he didn't paw it off his face. Reese kept the dog close at hand.

"Bring him along in the ambulance," Katy said.

Sam looked exasperated. "You know I can't bring a dog to the hospital."

"You can, trust me. Duke is highly trained. He won't be a problem. You can tell everyone he's Reese's therapy dog. Per ADA rules, they'll have to let him in."

"Okay, fine," Sam agreed with a heavy sigh. "But if there's any trouble once you arrive in the ER, keep me out of it."

"I'll make sure you don't get in trouble," Katy promised. Her throat was still sore, but the dull headache that had settled in the base of her skull seemed to be getting better with oxygen. Maybe putting the wet clothing over their faces had helped. She knew there were many potential long-term effects of severe smoke inhalation, especially if their lung tissue was badly scarred from the smoke.

But right now, she was happy to be alive. Safe from the fire and alive.

The ride to the hospital didn't take long at all, or maybe she'd slept for a good part of it. Now that the adrenaline rush had faded, her body felt as if she'd been run over by a truck. Exhaustion weighed on her limbs, and it seemed to take every ounce of strength she possessed just to lift her hand to adjust the oxygen mask on her face.

"What time is it?" she asked when Sam's face reappeared in her line of vision.

"Just past twelve thirty," Sam said. "We're going to have to secure the safety straps to get you out of the ambulance and into the ER, okay?"

"Sure." She kept her arms down along her sides and tried to remain still as Sam buckled the straps across her body. She took several deep breaths of oxygen, thinking how incredible it was that they'd only been in the woods for a few hours when it had seemed like a lifetime.

Sam and his colleague gently set the gurney on the ground and then hit the lever to bring it up to its full height. She craned her neck, trying to get a glimpse of Reese and Duke, but the other ambulance was just pulling in.

They wheeled her into the trauma bay, and she felt dizzy looking up at the bright lights overhead and hearing Sam recite her vital signs. She'd had no idea how vulnerable it felt to be a patient like this. She felt bad that she hadn't done more to reassure her patients in the past.

She wanted to protest that her condition wasn't serious enough to warrant being in the trauma bay, but when she tried to talk, no one was listening.

Since when did patients call the shots? Yeah, since never.

The straps across her chest loosened, and she looked up

to see Janelle leaning over her. "Hi, Dr. Katy, I'm just going to get you connected to the heart monitor, okay?"

She was embarrassed at the thought of being undressed in front of her colleagues, but Janelle did a good job of keeping her well covered as she connected the EKG leads.

"What's my pulse ox?" Katy asked. She wished she could see the display on the heart monitor, but it was located well behind her, out of view.

"A little on the low side, ninety percent right now," Janelle confirmed. "Apparently it was down as low as eighty-seven percent when Sam first checked it."

A normal reading would be closer to one hundred percent, but at least it was improving. She wondered how Reese was doing. She missed having him close by.

Hard to believe she'd only known him for a few days. It seemed much longer.

As the medical staff placed an IV, gave fluids, took blood and discussed x-rays, she battled a wave of helplessness.

She needed to see Reese. To make sure he and Duke were okay.

The thought of not seeing him again was painfully unbearable.

REESE WAS grateful Katy had insisted the ambulance crew provide oxygen to Duke and to bring him along, but he still wanted to find a vet. And soon.

He knew there was a small veterinary clinic located just outside Crystal Lake, but he had no idea if they were even open. Had people been evacuated from the town? Or did the firefighters have the blaze under control?

For the second time in three days, Reese found himself back in the trauma bay of the Hope County Hospital ER.

Only this time, Dr. Katy was in the spot next to him, rather than Marcus Boyle.

"Duke, stay," he ordered. Then he glanced up at the nurse hovering over him. "He won't hurt you," he said.

"I know. The paramedics told us you wouldn't get treatment without your dog," one of the nurses said. He blinked and tried to read her name tag. Merry, that was right. He remembered Merry now from the other night.

"He's well trained," Reese repeated. "And thanks for hooking him up to the oxygen too."

The medical staff gave Duke a wide berth but didn't seem overly concerned with having a dog nearby. He listened as they talked about him in the third person, as if he weren't right there, awake and conscious.

He turned his head to look over at Katy at the exact moment she glanced at him. He smiled at her from behind the oxygen mask and lifted a hand in acknowledgement.

He didn't want to think about the fact that this might be the last time he would see her for a while.

But he couldn't stay, no matter how much the doctors and nurses wanted him to. Even if getting Duke to the vet wasn't an option, he still needed to talk to his boss about the wildfire and his suspicions about the blond dude.

Reese tried to be patient, but it wasn't easy. They cleaned up the wound on his arm and placed fresh dressings over it. When they decided he needed a chest x-ray, he shook his head.

"Listen, Doc, I need to get out of here," he said, glaring at the ER physician on duty. He squinted to make out his name tag. Dr. Allen.

"Your pulse ox readings are getting better, but I highly recommend you stay on oxygen at least overnight, maybe even a few days," Dr. Allen said. "Not to mention, you could use at least three doses of IV antibiotics for your arm, just to make sure it doesn't get infected, but your lungs are the bigger concern right now. You're fortunate that you don't need hyperbaric treatments."

He had no idea what that meant, but it didn't matter. "Can't I get oxygen and antibiotics to go?" he asked. "I really need to take care of my dog and check in with my boss."

Dr. Allen narrowed his gaze. "Your dog is already getting some care. I'll make you a deal. You agree to a chest x-ray and IV antibiotics and I'll treat your dog, too. I can give him IV fluids in the scruff of his neck and keep the oxygen on for a while. How does that sound?"

Reese gave in. His dog was the most important issue right now. But he also needed to call his boss. "All right, Dr. Allen, you have a deal."

The doc waved a hand. "Call me Gabe. Now let's get that x-ray, so we can care for your dog."

The few minutes he was without oxygen didn't seem too bad, as they transferred him from the gurney to a wheelchair. But when they replaced the mask over his face, he couldn't deny that his breathing felt much better. He glanced at Duke, still wearing the face tent thingy around his neck. He was glad the dog didn't look too bad off. Maybe once he got some IV fluids in him, he'd be okay.

He didn't even want to think about what effect this injury might have on his career. Surely his breathing would get better, right? He wouldn't need oxygen forever, would he? Trekking through the woods with an oxygen tank wasn't exactly a viable option.

Pushing aside that pathetic image wasn't easy, but he told himself to concentrate on one issue at a time. Duke came first, and then he could worry about the rest. Besides, he should be glad they'd gotten safely out of the fire.

Praying with Katy had given him the determination to push on. He couldn't deny the power of faith.

The chest x-ray didn't take long, and as he was wheeled back to the trauma bay, he realized he could still lean on the power of prayer for healing, too.

His gut clenched when he saw the two sheriff's deputies waiting for him in the trauma bay. Deputy Armbruster and Deputy Kramer looked ill at ease, maybe because of the way Duke sat as still as a statue, as if waiting for the signal to attack.

He sighed and gave Duke the hand signal to lie down. The dog looked disappointed but stretched out on the floor.

"Deputies," he greeted them in his raspy voice. "What brings you here?"

"We need to ask you about the fire," Deputy Kramer said in a snide tone.

"Then why not talk to both of us?" Katy asked. Reese glanced over in surprise to find her in a wheelchair beside him. She must have come back from radiology, too.

The two deputies exchanged a look, and Reese could tell they weren't too happy with her idea.

Did they think she was going to lie to protect him?

"I'm afraid protocol dictates we'll need to talk to you separately," Deputy Armbruster said in a firm tone. "But we can split up if that makes you feel better."

It didn't, but Reese wanted to get this done and over with. "Fine. Where do you want to talk? I would think you'd want some privacy so we don't try to fix our stories."

"Gabe, are there two empty rooms for us to use?" Katy asked. "I'm sure you'd like to get the trauma bay cleaned up, anyway."

"Sure, take rooms eleven and twelve," Gabe said.

Katy wheeled herself toward a hallway that led farther

into the ER. He waited until Merry disconnected Duke from the oxygen regulator in the wall before he gave Duke the hand signal to come. The dog trotted along beside him.

Merry followed them into room eleven, connecting both his oxygen and Duke's back to the wall. She took a few extra minutes to hang his IV antibiotic before leaving. Reese was a little surprised that Deputy Armbruster took a seat across from him, leaving Katy to talk to Deputy Kramer. He relaxed a bit, trusting Armbruster would be more impartial.

Was it really just twelve hours ago that Kramer had accused him of breaking in to Katy's house? He could barely wrap his mind around it.

"Why don't you start at the beginning?" The way Armbruster sat back in his chair gave Reese the impression he actually intended to listen.

Reese had to think back to what had taken him out to the hiking trail in the first place. He reached over to sink his fingers into Duke's fur.

"Duke wanted to go out, and he headed straight for the hiking trail," Reese began. "I figured something was up, that maybe he'd caught the scent of the blond dude, so I let him take the lead."

"Just so I'm clear, the blond guy is the one you think was poaching with Boyle, correct?"

"Yes." Reese knew Kramer didn't believe him, but it was possible Armbruster was willing to keep an open mind. "I saw him several times when I was tracking Boyle, but I kept losing him."

"Go on," Deputy Armbruster encouraged.

"When I smelled the smoke, I thought Duke was tracking some careless campers, which was concerning since we've had such a dry spring."

"When did you run into Dr. Katy?"

"Duke found her." He stroked the dog's head. "I was going to head back up the trail in case there were people trapped up there, but then I saw the fire engulfed far too many trees, and I decided to get down to safety."

"And then what?"

"The fire surrounded us," Reese said in a grim tone. "We followed Duke to safety. He led us to water, and in the end, he brought the firefighters out to where we were."

There was a moment of silence before Deputy Armbruster cleared his throat. "That dog of yours is quite the hero."

"Yes. He is." Reese lifted his gaze. "I didn't see anyone, but I know that fire was started on purpose. A fire started by a campfire couldn't have surrounded us so quickly."

Armbruster nodded. "Yeah, that's what we think, too."

"Am I a suspect?" Reese asked.

"No." A ghost of a smile flashed over Armbruster's face. "I don't think you'd risk your dog."

Reese chuckled and then started coughing again. "No, I wouldn't. I wouldn't risk Katy, either."

"I know."

Reese felt as if a huge weight had been lifted from his shoulders. He wasn't a suspect anymore, at least not in Deputy Armbruster's eyes.

"Well, if that's all, I'd like to get Duke some treatments while we're here, although it would be better to get him in to see the vet as soon as possible."

"I hate to tell you, but the veterinary clinic isn't open," Deputy Armbruster said slowly.

"Because of the fire?" he asked.

"Yes. It's not just the vet that's closed. The entire town of Crystal Lake has been evacuated as a result of the fire,"

Armbruster said. "The roads have been closed off except for emergency vehicles."

Reese stared at him in shock. "Where did everyone go?"

"The Red Cross has set up tents a few miles outside of town. No one's going back home until we get the fire under control."

12

Katy stared at Deputy Kramer, trying to understand where he was coming from. "Reese didn't start the fire," she said firmly. "And I don't understand why you keep accusing him of doing all this stuff instead of trying to find the real culprit."

"You mentioned being surprised to see him on the trail," he persisted. "Why would you think that's a coincidence?"

"Why do you think he'd risk his own life?" she countered, getting angry. "Don't you understand? We almost died back there!"

Kramer's face flushed, and he stared down at his small notebook for several long seconds. "Is there anything else you can remember?" he finally asked.

"No." Katy didn't understand what Ian's problem with Reese was, but she was surprised at how eager he was to believe the worst. Which was strange because she'd worked with Ian before, and he'd always been great.

Now she couldn't wait for him to leave.

"All right, please call me if you remember anything more."

Yeah, right. "Sure," she agreed, which wasn't an outright lie. She'd call some other deputy if necessary, but not Ian Kramer.

After he left, she took several deep breaths in an attempt to calm down. Maybe it was Ian's job to believe the worst in people, but she didn't like the fact that he didn't seem to consider other possibilities.

Like the blond-haired man Reese had seen.

She was in the process of disconnecting her oxygen when Gabe walked into her room. "What are you doing?"

She winced, since there was no denying she'd been caught in the act. "Going over to make sure Reese is okay. Why? Are you here to discharge us?"

"Not exactly. I'm going to admit you both upstairs."

"Do you really think that's necessary?" she asked with a frown. "I'm sure you'll need those beds for real patients."

Gabe pinched the bridge of his nose as if she'd given him a headache. "Katy, you are a real patient, and so is Reese. Besides, you'll both be better off if you stay here since the town has been evacuated."

Her eyes widened at the news, and she wondered why she hadn't considered that earlier. "I'm not sure Reese will stay. He's worried about Duke."

"I've given the dog some fluids. I think he'll be fine."

"I didn't know that you were a practicing vet," she teased, feeling relieved to know Duke had gotten some care.

"I'm not, but thankfully, some of the basics are the same." Gabe took out his stethoscope to listen to her lungs. "Better, but not great."

"I know." She could feel the irritation in her nose and throat, and truthfully, staying on oxygen overnight was probably the right thing to do. "All right, I'll convince Reese we should stay."

"Good plan," Gabe agreed. "I'll get the orders placed, and then we'll get you both transported upstairs."

"Could we get scrubs? We're both in desperate need of a shower and a change of clothes."

"No problem." Gabe left the room, no doubt to find Reese. She finished disconnecting herself from the oxygen in the wall, transferring to the tank on the back of her wheelchair, and then wheeled herself over to join Reese. She could have walked but didn't have the portable oxygen tank on a wheeled carrier to use.

Deep down, she was glad they'd both have to stay the night at the hospital. Pathetic, really, that she was looking forward to spending more time with Reese before they went their separate ways.

"I need to call my boss," Reese was saying when she entered his room. "He needs all the help he can get right now."

"I don't think that's in your best interest, or Duke's, either," Gabe said in a stern tone. "You need oxygen, steroids, antibiotics, rest and fluids, in that order."

Reese scowled and then glanced down at Duke. She noticed the dog had a huge hump on his neck and wondered what had happened. "Is Duke hurt?" she asked.

"No, that's the fluid I injected," Gabe assured her. "It actually works very well. The fluid absorbs subcutaneously into their vascular system. I'll get him some medication, too. Maybe we can give it in some peanut butter or something."

She wasn't sure how Gabe knew how to take care of animals, but she was grateful he did.

"Reese, please stay, for Duke's sake."

He let out a heavy sigh and nodded. "All right, I'll stay. But only if Duke stays with me, and I'll need something to feed him. I doubt you stock pet supplies here."

"I can have Zack head out to get some dog food," Merry volunteered, walking into the room. "He keeps some in his car."

"Dishes, too," Reese added.

"Those I can find in the kitchen." Merry turned to Gabe. "Admission orders have been placed, and there are two inpatient beds available on three west, right next to each other."

Katy could feel her cheeks burn beneath the grime, and she wondered what Reese thought of the arrangements. She hadn't asked to have their rooms next to each other.

But she was secretly glad.

"Good. Call one of the techs to transport them up," Gabe directed. "I'll find clean scrubs for you both."

"Thanks, again, for everything," Reese said in a low voice. "I'm grateful for all the care you provided to Duke."

Gabe smiled. "It wasn't a problem. Easy enough since the dog didn't fight me. Did you train him yourself?"

"Yeah." Reese's smile was strained, and Katy found herself wondering if he'd gotten Duke right after his divorce. She could easily imagine Reese spending all his free time training Duke.

"I wouldn't mind getting a dog if you'd be willing to train him," Gabe continued. "Think about how much you'd charge and let me know."

Reese looked surprised at the offer. "Ah, okay. But you should know that most police-trained dogs go for several grand, so it's not cheap."

"I'd pay that much for a well-trained dog," Gabe mused. "My wife and I have two small children, so I wouldn't even consider a dog unless it was trained by someone who knew what he was doing. Like you."

Reese glanced at her, as if asking if he was for real. She smiled and nodded. Apparently training dogs for other people hadn't occurred to Reese before. And now he'd been handed the chance to make a little extra money.

She hoped he'd take it. Not for her sake but for his own. Because while she could care less about his debt, she knew it weighed heavily on his shoulders.

Reese was too proud to allow anyone else to pay off what he owed. And she figured Reese wouldn't even try to move forward with having a personal life until he'd gotten his financial situation under control.

Truthfully, she didn't mind waiting, if that's what it took. But would he give them a chance? She fully intended to find out.

Because at the moment, she couldn't imagine a future that didn't include Reese and Duke.

REESE TURNED the idea of training a dog for Gabe over and over in his mind as the young tech pushed him in his wheelchair up to his room. He'd never considered there to be a huge market for this type of thing, but obviously he was wrong.

But now that he thought about it, if he trained two dogs a year and kept up with his current frugal spending, he'd be out of debt sooner than he'd anticipated. Maybe even less than a year.

"Here's an admission kit with shampoo, toothbrush and shaving stuff in it," the tech said, pulling out a tub full of personal supplies. "Do you need me to hook up your dog to oxygen again?" The tech glanced at Duke in a way that made him think she might be afraid of the animal.

"I'll take care of it, thanks."

The tech shrugged and walked out of the room. He rose to his feet and took care of Duke before he took the tub of personal items and headed into the bathroom.

The face in the mirror looked far worse than he'd expected. The smoky smell seemed to be imbedded in his airway, and he hoped that taking a shower and changing his clothes would help.

A knock at the door startled him. "Mr. Webster? My name is Amy, and I'll be your nurse. I have clean scrubs here for you to wear."

"Thanks." He opened the door and gratefully took the scrubs.

She frowned. "Did you disconnect your own IV?"

"Yeah. Can't you wait until I finish showering before you hook it back up?"

"I guess, but I also need to put a waterproof dressing over your arm."

"Okay."

Amy quickly wrapped his arm. "Call me when you're finished," she said.

"I will," he promised before closing the bathroom door.

When he emerged a good forty-five minutes later, he felt a lot better. The smoke smell still lingered but not nearly as powerful as it was before. He'd used the cheap razor they'd provided without nicking himself too badly, and he was happy to be wearing clean clothes.

He debated giving Duke a bath, since the dog's fur still smelled like smoke, but decided against trying that feat in the shower. It was difficult enough in a bathtub.

He pressed the call button, and soon Amy returned. "Wow, you look great!"

"Thanks." Actually, he felt like a fraud staying here in

the hospital when all he needed were antibiotics, steroids and oxygen. But when he stretched out on the bed, he realized just how tired he was.

Strange to be so exhausted when he was used to hiking for hours in the woods.

Amy cleaned and reconnected the IV tubing to the catheter in his arm. "I've called for a late lunch tray. It should be here soon."

"Thanks." He glanced over at Duke, who was once again stretched out on the floor beside his bed. "Don't worry. Hopefully your food will be here soon."

Duke's tail thumped against the side of his bed, making him smile.

He hoped Merry made good on her promise. Duke deserved the best. While he waited, he used the phone to call his boss. Unfortunately, Gavin didn't answer. Leaving a message didn't feel right, but what else could he do? No doubt, Gavin was out at the scene of the fire.

Where he should be, too. Making sure the blond dude didn't get away with attempted murder.

Too bad he still had no clue as to the blond dude's identity, which made it difficult to know where to find him.

AFTER CLEANING up and eating the tray of food that arrived courtesy of her nurse, Katy stared out the window, fighting the urge to go over to talk to Reese.

No sense in pushing her company on him. Heaven knew they'd spent over half a day together. No doubt he was appreciating some time alone.

She closed her eyes and tried to rest, but despite her lack of sleep the night before and her bone-deep exhaustion, sleep eluded her.

Another hour dragged by, and finally she gave up and crawled out of bed. She didn't want to use the wheelchair—bad enough to be a patient—so she connected her oxygen to a portable wheeling tank to take with her.

The door to Reese's room was partially closed, and for a moment, she stood uncertainly. Just because she couldn't sleep didn't mean he wasn't.

She'd turned around to head back to her room when she heard him talking. "Gavin, please call me as soon as you get this message. Thanks."

Okay, so he wasn't sleeping. Taking a deep breath to bolster her courage, she lightly tapped on the door. "Reese? It's Katy."

"Come in," he called. His voice was still a little hoarse, just like hers.

"Hi, how's Duke?" She really did care about the dog, even though it was also an easy excuse for her being there.

"He's good. Wow, you look great." The warmth in Reese's gaze made her toes curl.

"Thanks, so do you. Although I can't seem to get rid of the smoke smell," she said, wrinkling her nose.

"Well, you might want to keep your distance from Duke, then, because I haven't given him a bath yet, and his fur still reeks from the fire."

"It's not his fault," she said, sitting in the chair beside his bed. She leaned over and rubbed Duke's fur, wondering again how she could ever have been afraid of him. "Did your boss call you back yet?"

He grimaced and shook his head. "Not yet. Sitting around here is driving me crazy. I feel like I should be out at the scene of the fire."

"I didn't realize that DNR game wardens were also trained as firefighters."

"We have some training, but not to the extent the smoke jumpers do," he admitted. "Still, I'd rather be near the action."

"I get it," Katy said with a sigh. "I'm not used to being at loose ends, either. I keep thinking about the patients who are probably coming in for treatment. I'm sure Gabe could use help, yet here I am, doing nothing."

"You're resting and getting better," he pointed out.

She lifted a brow. "So are you. And so is Duke."

"Touché," he said with a wry smile. But then his gaze turned serious. "I'm sorry you had to get mixed up in all this."

"It's not your fault," she reminded him. "And trust me, I made sure that Deputy Kramer was crystal clear on my opinion."

Reese scowled. "You mean he still thinks I'm involved?"

Maybe she shouldn't have brought the subject up. "I'm sure it's just his usual suspicious nature."

Reese didn't look convinced. "Funny, Armbruster didn't seem to share his opinion. In fact, he told me straight up that I wasn't a suspect."

"Really? That's wonderful!" Katy was thrilled and relieved to hear it. "I'm sure Devon will talk some sense into Ian."

"You're on a first-name basis with him, huh?"

She frowned. "Well, yeah, sort of. I see the deputies all the time, and last year I took care of Devon after he was injured. Ian was there the whole time, so I guess it was natural to call him by his first name."

"Maybe he just doesn't like the way you're always defending me," Reese pointed out. "He might believe the gossip circling around town."

"What, you mean, like, he's jealous? Don't be ridiculous. There's absolutely nothing like that between us."

"Maybe he'd like there to be something more," Reese said in a low voice. "He's not a bad guy, seems to have a solid career."

Her stomach clenched painfully as she realized Reese was trying to subtly tell her that he wasn't interested.

As if the closeness between them, and that heated kiss, hadn't happened.

As if she didn't already care about him, obviously more than she should.

"I'm not interested in Ian that way," she said, forcing herself to meet his gaze head on. "You're the first man I've kissed in well over a year."

A strained silence fell between them, making her wish she'd held her tongue.

"Knock, knock," a female voice called out, breaking the moment. "Reese? Are you decent?"

Katy froze for a second, but then recognized Merry's voice. Merry popped into the room, a half-full bag of dog food in her arms.

"Hi, Merry," Reese greeted her warmly. Katy wondered if he realized that Merry was married to Deputy Zack Crain. "Thanks so much for bringing Duke's dinner."

"You're welcome, and actually, Zack's the one who brought it in." She set the bag down and pulled two silver bowls out. "Do you want me to fill these for you?"

"I can get it," Reese protested, swinging his scrub-clad legs over the side of the bed. "But thanks, anyway."

"Sounds good. Hey, Dr. Katy, how are you feeling?" Merry asked.

"I'm fine. Should be back to work tomorrow."

Merry grinned and shook her head. "I know it's not

easy to be on the wrong side of a hospital bed, but there's no reason to rush back to work. We have it all under control."

Katy smiled, remembering how Merry had suffered a concussion last year after being hit by one of their psych patients. "I'll be back to work tomorrow," she repeated.

"You can fight that out with Gabe," Merry said with a wave of her hand. "I have to run, but let me know if you need anything else, okay?"

The room seemed painfully quiet after Merry left, despite the crunching sounds from Duke enjoying his dinner.

Katy thought that Reese might be trying to avoid a personal conversation, so she rose to her feet and grabbed her oxygen tank. "I'm almost out of air. Have a good night, Reese."

His smile seemed strained. "You, too, Katy. And don't go back to work too soon, okay?"

"I won't." She kept her gaze focused on maneuvering the oxygen tank as she returned to her room.

She crawled beneath the covers, wishing she could forget the awkward conversation with Reese. Her throat felt thick with tears. Ridiculous to cry over a man she barely knew.

So why did she feel so miserable?

Katy closed her eyes and opened her heart and her mind to God. She needed to believe that God had a plan for her, even if she didn't understand what it entailed.

She slept fitfully, getting up several times, not used to hearing the hospital sounds from a patient's perspective. Not that the staff were exceptionally noisy or anything.

She heard a thud when she came out of the bathroom, and she stood for a minute, trying to figure out what was wrong. Had Reese fallen to the floor? Or maybe some other patient had fallen?

The door of her room abruptly swung open, and she stumbled backward in surprise when a tall blond-haired man entered her room. He was wearing scrubs but didn't look at all familiar. He wasn't wearing a name tag, either.

A chill snaked down her spine. Was this the guy who Reese had seen in the woods?

He took another step into the room, and that's when she saw the gun clutched in his right hand. "If you scream, I'll shoot," he said in a flat tone.

She swallowed hard and nodded. Oh, yeah, she believed him. "Who are you?" she asked in a whisper.

"That doesn't matter. You're going to do exactly as I say, understand?"

The chill congealed into ice. She licked her suddenly dry lips. "O-okay."

"You're going to come with me," the blond guy said in that eerily calm voice. "I'm going to keep you directly in front of me so that game warden can't sic that dog of his on me."

Katy didn't want to do as he asked, but what choice did she have? If she'd been closer to her bed, she could use the call light to call the nurse, but she wasn't.

She wanted to believe there was a way to use her brain to get away from the blond guy, but she hesitated a moment too long. Suddenly he was right beside her, grabbing her arm in a grip so painful she felt tears sting her eyes.

"Don't even think about trying anything stupid," he said in a low voice.

Her throat was so tight with fear she couldn't speak. She gave a brief nod, indicating she understood.

"Let's go." He pressed the gun into her side.

She walked slowly toward the doorway, hoping and praying that Reese would figure out a way to get them out of this mess.

Before this maniac killed them both, and poor Duke, too.

13

A low growl from Duke awakened Reese from a restless sleep. How on earth anyone managed to sleep in a hospital bed was beyond him. Of course, the fact that Duke was sleeping on the foot of the mattress didn't help. The hospital bed definitely wasn't big enough for the two of them.

But he'd refused to make Duke stay on the hard floor. Not after the way he'd saved his life. He was glad that the dog had been given the same meds he'd been given, just in a smaller dose.

"What's wrong, boy?" he whispered.

Duke had lifted his head and was staring intently at the doorway. Was someone out there? Duke hadn't growled when the nurse had come in a few hours ago to check his blood pressure and to hang another dose of the IV antibiotic. She'd also checked the oxygen level in his blood. His readings continued to improve, which was good news.

Reese swung his legs over the edge of the bed and slowly rose to his feet. He was hampered a bit by the IV tubing and resisted the urge to pull the stupid catheter out. He hadn't gotten very far when he heard someone call his name.

"Reese?" The whisper sounded like Katy, although that didn't make sense because Duke knew Katy's scent and wouldn't growl at her.

"I'm awake," he said in a low voice. "Come in. Is something wrong?"

The door to his room swung open at the same time Duke rose off the bed, the growl in his throat growing louder. It took a minute for him to realize that Katy wasn't alone. The blond dude was standing almost directly behind her.

"Call off your dog, or I'll kill her."

"Down, Duke." The frightened expression in Katy's eyes ripped at his heart, and based on the awkward angle the guy had on her, he realized the blond dude was holding a gun pressed against her side. His stomach clenched, and he took a deep breath, trying to remain calm. "Duke won't attack unless I give the command. What do you want?"

For several long seconds, the blond guy didn't say anything. Even though it was dark in his room, the muted light from the hall revealed the guy was wearing scrubs.

"We're going to take care of the dog first," the blond stranger said.

"Wait, why are you doing this? I don't even know your name! What's the point of killing us?"

Reese couldn't make out the expression in the blond guy's eyes in the dim light, but his cold, flat tone was not reassuring.

"I have no choice. Boyle would have eventually ratted me out, and you wouldn't stop searching for me."

Reese still didn't understand, but he wanted to keep him talking, hoping someone might come down the hall to find them. "I might not have kept searching for you if you hadn't smashed my truck."

"I needed to keep you from going back into the woods to find the cougar."

Okay, the way this guy answered every question in that same emotionless tone was really eerie. Why was he acting like some sort of robot?

"Look, no one has to die here tonight," Reese said. "I'm sure we can work something out."

"I disagree. Once you're out of my way, I can go back to living in the woods without interference."

Reese had always suspected the guy was ex-military, and seeing him up close only confirmed his original impression. He wished he understood what was going on in his mind. Did he really think that he could kill two people and a dog without being caught? Was he poaching to live off the land to stay off grid? And if so, why kill a cougar?

Unless Boyle had decided to kill the cougar on his own? Suddenly it made sense. "You were tracking Boyle, the same way I was," he said slowly. "You weren't working together at all. You were upset with Boyle because he was drawing unwanted attention from the DNR."

"Too smart for your own good."

Reese would have felt better if there had been satisfaction in his tone, but there wasn't.

How could he get through to the blond guy if he didn't feel anything? There wasn't a hint of emotion for him to exploit. Nothing that Reese could appeal to in order to make him change his mind.

"Dog first," he repeated. He let go of Katy's arm for a brief moment and pulled something out of the pocket of his scrubs. He tossed the syringe on the bedside table and quickly resumed his tight grip on Katy's arm. "Inject him with the contents of that syringe. Don't worry, the sedative will act quickly, and he'll die a painless death."

Reese stared at the syringe and then dragged his gaze up to meet Katy's. Her mouth was pulled together in a terse frown, and she gave her head a slight shake.

She winced as the blond guy pressed the gun painfully into her side. "Don't make me shoot all three of you. Gunshot wounds hurt. But if that's truly the way you want to go, that's fine with me. I can shoot all three of you and still find a way to escape. I won't be taken prisoner again."

Reese stepped forward and picked up the syringe, his thoughts whirling. Again? Had this guy been captured during the war in Afghanistan? Was that what had messed with his mind?

"Let us go, and I'll make sure that you can resume living off the land where no one will bother you," he said, making one last effort. "I promise that you don't have to kill us in order to get away."

"I'll count to three. If you haven't injected the dog by then, I'll start shooting. One..."

Reese wished he knew what was in the syringe. If he only gave a partial dose, would Duke still die? Could he find a way to pretend to inject him? But if Duke didn't go down, then the blond guy would know he'd faked it.

"Two..."

"Okay, stop counting. I'll do it." He stepped closer to Duke and put his left arm around the dog's neck. Tears burned his eyes as he lifted the syringe.

"I love you, Duke," he whispered.

"Jesse, don't! Let her go!"

Reese froze and glanced up in surprise to see Ian Kramer standing in the doorway of his room. The deputy was wearing full SWAT gear and held his gun trained on the blond dude, who still held Katy in a tight grip. It dawned on Reese that the two men had similar facial features, although Ian Kramer's hair was as dark as Jesse's was light. Still, now that he saw them together, he wondered why he hadn't noticed the resemblance before.

They looked similar enough to be brothers.

"Go away, Ian. This isn't your business." Jesse didn't as much as glance at the deputy.

"I didn't want to believe you were involved in this, Jesse." Ian Kramer looked upset, but the tip of his gun didn't waver. "I turned my back on the illegal hunting, knowing how important it was for you to be independent and live off the land. But you went too far when you tried to run them off the road, which I figured out when I ran the license plate tag. Then you set that fire. And now murder? What are you thinking? You know I can't let you get away with this."

Reese palmed the syringe and edged a little closer to Jesse. He wanted to imbed the syringe into Jesse, but he couldn't risk the gun going off and killing Katy.

"You won't kill me," Jesse said in that same eerie voice. "You love me, remember? You told me that at least a dozen times while I was recuperating from being held prisoner."

"I do love you, Jesse. You're my brother. That's why I can't let you do this. Don't you see? There's no point in killing them if we have you surrounded. You can't escape. Please surrender your weapon. I'll make sure you get the help you need."

"The only thing that helps me is to be alone in the woods with nothing surrounding me."

"I know, Jesse. I'll find a way to make that happen. I promise I'll do everything in my power to help you."

Reese wanted to believe the deputy was getting through

to Jesse. Had his hand loosened its grip on the gun pressed against Katy's side? He inched closer.

"Okay, here's another idea," Ian said, sounding desperate. "Use me as your hostage. We can leave the hospital, and I'll take you someplace safe."

Reese held his breath as Jesse seemed to seriously consider the idea. "The other deputies won't let me through, not if I have you."

"Trust me, they will." Ian's voice oozed confidence. "Especially if I tell them to."

"I need to go far away," Jesse said. "The other side of the country if necessary. Maybe Alaska."

"We will. I promise."

Ian glanced at Reese for an intense moment, and he understood the silent message. Ian wanted Reese to use the sedative in the syringe to subdue Jesse.

He gave an almost imperceptible nod. He wished he knew what was in the syringe and tried to squeeze some of the contents out without attracting attention. Duke weighed 95 pounds, and Jesse was obviously closer to two hundred. Surely a half dose wouldn't be as lethal?

"Let her go, Jesse. Katy, I want you to go over to the opposite side of the room, understand?"

"Yes," Katy agreed softly.

Reese tensed and sent up a silent prayer for strength as he prepared to jump. He watched for the moment when Jesse released Katy, then lunged forward and stabbed the syringe into Jesse's thigh.

"No," Katy shouted but he pressed on the plunger at the same time Ian grabbed Jesse's gun. The big blond man let out an animal-like howl as he dropped to his knees.

"Get back. He needs medical attention," Katy shouted. "Call a code blue!"

Reese flipped on the lights. Ian used his radio to call for help. Less than sixty seconds later, the room was flooded with people, mostly deputies.

"Lift him onto the bed," Katy snapped from where she knelt on the floor next to Jesse. "Then I want everyone out of here except medical personnel. I need room to work."

Reese snagged Ian's arm. "Get one of the nurses in here to help her."

Ian left the room and returned with several nurses. A few minutes later, Gabe Allen joined them. Katy pretty much ignored him, barking orders like a drill sergeant.

"I want a full set of labs drawn, including heavy metals. I want an IV going wide open to flush out his system. I want an intubation tray in case we lose his airway. Amy, see if there's any way to get a dialysis unit called in."

Reese was impressed at how quickly the nursing staff jumped to do her bidding.

"He's not breathing," one of the nurses announced.

"Where's that intubation tray?"

"Right here." One of the nurses thrust the tray onto the bedside table.

"He could have used a paralytic combined with a sedative," Gabe said as Katy grabbed equipment from the bin. "That's the most painless way to kill someone."

"Let's hope so," Katy mumbled. "At least I know how to treat that."

With deft skill, she placed the breathing tube with Gabe's assistance.

"We need to get him to the ICU," Gabe said. "We can continue to treat him for the unknown substance better with monitoring equipment."

"Dialysis would be his best option," Katy said with a

sigh. "Especially since we don't know what he had in that syringe."

"There's two more syringes in his pocket," Amy said, holding them up. "We could ask the lab to test the contents."

"Good job," Katy said with a grim smile. "The only problem is that getting them tested will take time."

Reese glanced at Ian, who looked sick to his stomach with the news.

Time was one thing Jesse didn't have.

KATY WANTED to follow Jesse up to the ICU, but Gabe refused to let her. "You're still a patient, and it's not even dawn yet. Go back to bed and get some sleep."

She watched as they left, wheeling Jesse on a stretcher. She lingered in Reese's room, waiting for the nurses to finish putting everything back in order. It didn't take long, and soon they were alone.

"I can't believe it's finally over," Reese said, sitting on the edge of his bed with a sigh. "And now I understand why Kramer was trying to pin this on me. He didn't want to face the fact that his brother was the guilty one."

"I feel bad for Jesse," Katy admitted. She sat down in the empty chair located near the bed. "It's obvious he's been traumatized."

"Yeah, I know. I feel bad for him, too. But at the same time, I know he would have made good on his threat to kill us."

She suppressed a shiver. "You're right. I've never been so scared in my entire life."

Duke made a high-pitched sound in the back of his throat, grabbing Reese's attention. "I think he needs to go outside."

"I understand." Katy reluctantly rose to her feet. "I'll see you in the morning, okay?"

"Sure." Reese surprised her by reaching over and embracing her in a big hug. "I'm glad you're okay," he whispered.

"I'm glad you're okay, too," she whispered back.

She relished his embrace, but of course, it was over too soon. He released her and stepped back. "We'll talk more tomorrow."

Hope filtered into her heart. "Sounds good."

She waited as Reese disconnected himself from the oxygen tubing and the IV so he could take Duke outside to relieve himself.

She headed back into her room and put her oxygen back on before climbing into bed. She hadn't even noticed her breathing while she'd been held captive by Jesse Kramer.

But now that she had her oxygen back on, she could tell her breathing was a little easier. She closed her eyes and somehow managed to fall asleep.

Bright sunlight streamed in through the window, waking her up bright and early. She peered at the clock, thankful to realize she'd slept at least for a few hours.

She slid out of bed, freshened up in the bathroom and then poked her head out of her room. Reese's door was closed, so rather than bothering him, she flagged down a nurse.

"Would you please get me a fresh oxygen tank so I can walk up to the ICU?" she asked. "I want to check on my patient."

The nurse lifted a brow, as if questioning the use of the pronoun. Hmm. Could she have a patient when she was a patient herself? Probably not.

"I'm friends with his brother," she clarified, although it was a bit of a stretch. "Please?"

"I'll get you the oxygen, but you should know that the guy is a prisoner patient, so they might not let you up to see him."

Katy nodded. "Okay, thanks for the warning."

The nurse returned a few minutes later with a fresh oxygen tank in a wheeled carrier. She hooked herself up and then walked down the hall to the elevators. Normally she preferred the stairs, but the oxygen tank took that decision out of her hands.

The ICU was located one floor up. She walked in and immediately saw the deputy sitting outside one of the rooms. No doubt, Jesse's room.

She recognized Deputy Thomas and gave him a nod. "Hi there. How is he doing?"

"About the same," Deputy Thomas said. "Still not conscious."

She gestured to the door. "Do you mind if I go in to see him? I promise I won't stay long."

The deputy grimaced and shook his head. "Prisoner patients aren't allowed visitors. I've already bent the rule for his brother."

Katy smiled. "Yes, but I'm not a visitor, I'm a doctor. I'm the one who put in the breathing tube. I just want to check on his condition."

"Okay, fine, you get five minutes."

"Thanks." She went into the room and noticed that Ian was sitting beside the bed, asleep in the chair, despite the no-visitor rule. She tiptoed farther into the room, trying not to disturb him.

She glanced up at the monitoring equipment, relieved to

notice that his vital signs appeared stable. What had been in that syringe? What if he never woke up?

"I'm sorry, Dr. Katy," Ian said in a low voice.

She glanced at him in surprise. "I think you need to apologize to Reese more than to me."

"I know." Ian scrubbed his hands over his face. "If I had known how bad Jesse was..."

She nodded, understanding his dilemma. "Has he shown any signs of waking up?" she asked.

"Not yet." Ian stared at his brother. "I'm not sure which is worse, having him stay like this or being arrested and sent to jail."

She wasn't sure what to say to that. She sensed that for Jesse, jail would be the worse option.

Ian knew that, too.

"I'll check back later," she assured him. She left the room and walked down the hall, anxious to talk to the nurse caring for Jesse. She wanted to know how his kidneys were doing and if any of the lab work had come back abnormal.

She stood in front of the nurse's desk, waiting for the unit clerk to get off the phone, when a harried woman came rushing toward her.

"You! This is all your fault!" the woman accused harshly. "My son is brain-dead, and it's all your fault!"

Katy froze, staring at the woman in horror. What on earth was she talking about? She'd never seen this woman before in her life.

"I'm sorry to hear about your son, but I think you must have me confused with someone else," Katy said gently.

The woman's face twisted into a mask of pure hatred. "I know exactly who you are," she spat. "You're the doctor who killed my Danny. Danny Truitt was your patient, and you sent him home too soon. Now he's dead! They're taking him off life support!"

The blood drained from her face as she remembered taking care of Danny Truitt, the young man who'd been extremely intoxicated and stabbed with a knife. She'd gotten sidetracked when the gunshot victims had been brought in, but she knew she'd given orders to discharge Danny only when he'd been awake and his vitals had been stable.

Was it possible she was responsible for discharging him too early? Just like she'd discharged Steffie too soon, when she'd been back in Baltimore?

Was she really responsible for the death of another patient?

14

No. *This couldn't be happening. Not again. Please, Lord, not again!*

Katy reached out for the wall as the room spun around her. In the deepest portion of her mind, she noticed one of the nurses had ushered Danny's mother away.

Is it true? Dear Lord, are her accusations true? Did I fail another one of my patients?

"Katy, sit down." Reese came over and put his arm around her shoulders, but she shrank away from his touch.

The fact that Reese had heard everything only made matters worse. He'd run in the other direction if he knew the truth. And she wouldn't blame him.

"I—can't. Leave me alone. I need to go." Somehow she managed to slide away from him. She grabbed the handle of her oxygen tank and forced her legs to carry her toward the door.

She stumbled down the hallway to the elevator. Leaning heavily against the wall, she waited for the doors to open. She rode back down to the nursing unit where her room was located but headed into the nurse's station and sank down at the closest computer station.

With trembling fingers, she entered her password and opened Danny Truitt's electronic medical record. Tears burned in her eyes, blurring the words on the screen. She swiped them away with the back of her hand and tried to focus on reading the most recent progress notes.

Her heart sank when she realized that at least part of the woman's accusations were true. Danny had been readmitted twelve hours after Katy had discharged him from the ER right at the end of her shift. She reviewed the discharge information. The nurses had documented well. She remembered Danny had been awake and belligerent, demanding to go home. He'd also been demanding pain medication. Not entirely unreasonable, since he had been stabbed. She remembered, now, telling the nurses to go ahead and discharge him.

He'd seemed well enough to leave, and since he was an adult, they couldn't keep him against his will. They'd given enough fluids to help bring down his alcohol level. So what had happened over the next twelve hours? Why had he been brought back to the hospital?

A sick sense of dread enveloped her as she read through Danny's subsequent ER note. He'd been found down and completely unresponsive by his roommates. They'd started CPR and gotten him to the hospital but too late.

He'd suffered severe brain damage.

She slumped forward, burying her face in her hands. Danny's case was different from Steffie's, but the end result was the same.

Only this time, she didn't have a high patient load and understaffing to blame for the mistake.

The blame was hers alone.

REESE DIDN'T UNDERSTAND what was going on in Katy's mind, but it was obvious the woman's wild accusations had caused Katy to withdraw into herself. He'd followed her back down to the nursing unit and watched her from the hallway as she peered at one of the computer screens.

Surely she didn't believe the kid's medical issues were her fault? From what the nurse in the ICU had said, it sounded more like the kid had overdosed on his pain meds. That couldn't be Katy's fault.

He watched her collapse in front of the computer and decided this had gone on long enough. Ignoring the openly curious expressions on the staff members' faces, he strode behind the desk and went over to Katy.

"Come on, Katy. Let's go. You can't stay here like this."

She didn't acknowledge him verbally or meet his gaze but must have heard him since she rose to her feet. He wanted to put his arm around her but didn't dare, not after the way she'd recoiled from him in the ICU. Careful not to get too close, he stayed behind her as she made her way down the hall toward her room. He wracked his brain for a way to break through the wall she'd built between them.

She walked into her room and sat down on the edge of her bed, staring down at her feet, despair etched on her features.

"Katy, please don't do this to yourself," he urged, sitting in the chair across from her. "That boy's mother is lashing out in her grief. It's not your fault he overdosed on his pain medications."

She swallowed hard and raised her tortured gaze to his. "He came in highly intoxicated. Maybe I shouldn't have given him any pain meds."

"Would you have given any other stab wound patient pain meds?" he pressed. "How many stitches did you put in, anyway?"

"Fourteen," she whispered. "And don't you understand? I have to take each patient's individual history into account before making a medical decision. Knowing that he tended to abuse alcohol means it's not a stretch that he might do the same with pain meds."

He couldn't pretend to understand what the right medical decision would have been, but he still didn't see how she could feel responsible for the kid's overdose.

"Katy, you're a good doctor. You've saved countless patients' lives, including Boyle's. Remember how you saved Jacob from drowning? You were the one who encouraged me to believe in God's plan, remember?"

She nodded but didn't say anything.

"I turned my back on God until you showed me the way back to my faith. While we were stuck on the trail in the woods, I realized that if Suzanne hadn't left me and cleaned out our bank account, I wouldn't have Duke. I wouldn't be a DNR game warden, a job I love. And I wouldn't have met you. I understand that, right now, it's hard to understand why Danny ended up back here, but I have to believe that there's a reason."

Katy's eyes filled with tears. "What if the reason is to tell me I'm not fit to be a doctor? That maybe I should do something else with my life?"

He reached over and took both of her hands in his. "You don't really believe that. Not after all the lives you've saved. You told me that you helped take care of Devon Armbruster last year when he was injured. Don't you think that Danny's situation is more likely a message to other kids his age?"

She drew in a choppy breath. "The reason I left Baltimore General to come here was because of another patient death. Her name was Steffie Moore, and she was only eighteen years old. She came in with belly pain but got better with fluids, so I discharged her. But she actually had a burst appendix. She died because of me. And now Danny is dead, too. All because of me."

He wasn't sure what to say to that, other than he didn't believe either of the patients' outcomes were her fault. "Did the hospital blame you for Steffie's death?"

"No."

"Was there a lawsuit filed against you?"

"Not yet. But there's still time. I dread opening my mail every day, thinking that I'll find the summons and complaint."

"Katy, even good doctors get sued sometimes. I wish I could help you believe this isn't your fault."

"It's not her fault," Gabe said from the doorway. He strode into Katy's room, scowling at her. "Listen to me. Danny's roommates confessed that they saw Danny taking pills and drinking alcohol. They admitted he passed out on the sofa and they thought he'd sleep it off. It wasn't until one of the kids went over to wake him up that they realized he wasn't breathing. Danny's mother is just looking for someone to blame."

"Really?" Katy looked up at Gabe with hope shimmering in her eyes. "You don't think it's my fault for discharging him with pain meds?"

Gabe snorted. "Yeah, like you wouldn't be in worse trouble if you'd refused to give pain meds to a patient with a stab wound. It's not your fault the kid had a huge drinking problem. And I'm sure his mother knows that."

"Maybe, but I still have Steffie's death on my conscience," Katy murmured.

"Don't you think I feel guilty over stabbing Jesse with that syringe?" Reese spoke up. "Especially when he's up there fighting for his life? We're only human. We all make mistakes. God forgives us our sins. Why can't you?"

"Reese is right," Gabe added.

Katy nodded slowly. "I know you're both right. It's just easier said than done."

"Having faith, believing in God's will, handling the ups and downs of life—all of that is easier said than done," Reese reminded her.

A glimmer of a smile toyed with her mouth. "I'll try," she said softly.

"Good. The reason I came up here is to let you know that I've covered your shift, so you have the day off," Gabe announced.

"Thank you. I'll make it up to you sometime soon," Katy said.

"The doctor came by while you were upstairs," Reese added. "He's planning to discharge us both, although he said he needed to examine you first. He should be back any minute."

"That's good, even if we can't go home yet," Katy said.

"You can go home. Sheriff Torretti made the announcement earlier today. After working all night, they managed to put the fire out, and it looks as if there were only a few houses damaged as a result. Everyone else has been permitted to return to their homes."

"I'm so glad to hear that," Katy admitted.

Reese nodded in agreement, although, deep down, he hated knowing that his time with Katy was coming to an end.

He wanted to see her again, but there was still his debt to consider. Even with adding dog training as a way to earn extra income, he still had several months before he'd have the debt paid off.

So maybe this was for the best. As much as he cared about Katy, he didn't have anything to offer her. Not until he was free of debt. No, it was better for her to get on with her life, especially now that the danger was over.

He and Duke would head home. Too bad the log cabin that had once been his sanctuary now only seemed lonely without someone to share it with.

Someone like Katy.

THE DAYS PASSED without Katy seeing any sign of Reese, although he occupied her thoughts constantly. Almost daily, she battled the urge to drive out to the log cabin he shared with Duke to see how they were doing.

She couldn't keep lying to herself. She loved him. Even though they were opposites on many levels, she still loved him.

But she knew he didn't feel the same way. Or maybe it was more accurate to say he wouldn't let himself feel the same way. And while she understood, she also felt sad that he wouldn't at least talk to her about it.

She had to honor his decision, even if she didn't agree.

Spending her free time in church, talking privately to Pastor John, had helped her overcome some of her guilt related to Danny's and Steffie's deaths. Just like back in Baltimore, the quality committee at Hope County Hospital hadn't found her decision making to be at fault.

But she still mourned the fact that two young people had died far too young.

And she often agonized over any discharge that was even a slight bit questionable.

On Wednesday morning, exactly one week after she and Reese had been discharged from the hospital, Katy sat on her porch, staring out over the lake. Only half the woods behind the lake were intact. The rest of the trees had blackened limbs in the aftermath of the fire.

Crystal Lake's income from tourism had taken a hit, although people were still coming to the lake. Despite the annoying crowds and extra workload at the hospital, Katy joined in with the rest of the parishioners, praying for their tourism to return to previous levels.

They prayed for Ian and Jesse Kramer too. Jesse had woken up and was getting psychiatric treatment, but he'd already tried to escape twice, desperate for the freedom of the woods.

"Hi, Katy."

She glanced over to see Reese walking across her lawn toward her with Duke at his side. Her heart filled with a mixture of elation and relief.

He'd finally come to see her!

"Hi, Reese. Hi, Duke."

Reese gave the dog a hand gesture, and Duke came running over to her, his entire body shaking with glee. She bent over to give him a good rub, dodging the licks he aimed at her face.

"Down, Duke," Reese said mildly. "She doesn't want your dog slobber all over her."

"I missed you," she murmured. She glanced up at Reese. "I missed both of you."

"We missed you, too." Reese seemed a little off-balance as he stood there watching her. "I—um, stopped by the hospital, but you weren't working today."

"No, today's my day off." Her previous elation began to waver. "Why? Is something wrong?"

"No, it's just, I think it's been ten days, and I need to get these sutures out. The angle is too awkward to do it myself, and they're itching like crazy."

"Sutures," she repeated, her cheeks flushing with embarrassment. So he hadn't actually come to see her on a personal level. He just needed his stitches removed.

Disappointment stabbed deeply, but she bent her head, hoping he wouldn't notice. "Well, come inside then. Lucky for you, I have a first aid kit here that should do the trick."

"Stay, Duke," Reese said as she opened the back door.

"It's okay, he can come inside," Katy hastened to reassure him. "Has the vet checked him out?"

"Yes, apparently Dr. Allen's treatment was exactly what he needed. What about you?" Reese followed her into the kitchen. "Are you all right?"

"I still have bouts of shortness of breath with exertion, but otherwise I'm fine." Katy pulled out her first aid kit and then gestured toward the table. "Have a seat."

Reese sat down in the kitchen chair and pulled the short sleeve of his T-shirt out of the way so she could see his wounds. The scent of Reese's aftershave teased her senses, and she had to force herself to stay focused on his incisions.

"These suture lines look pretty good, considering everything you went through," she said.

"Thanks to you," he said in a low voice.

She didn't know what to say to that, so she pulled the small scissors and tweezers from the kit and began to snip and pull the sutures free.

"There, all finished," she said, striving for a light tone. "I'm just going to put some antibiotic ointment on it for now, but you should be fine from here. If the wound opens at all, you'll need to come back to the ER for care."

"Thanks, Katy." He rose to his feet, and she took a step back, needing some distance.

"No problem." She hoped he didn't notice the husky note in her tone. She turned toward the table, intending to clean up, but he captured her hand in his, holding her in place. She glanced up in surprise.

"The sutures were just an excuse to come and see you," Reese said. "I've missed you so much. I know that I don't have anything to offer you, but I can't seem to stay away."

"Oh, Reese, you have a lot to offer. You have your heart."

His gaze softened, and he subtly pulled her closer. "You've mended my broken heart, so I guess it's only fair I give it to you. I love you, Katy. More than I thought possible."

Sheer joy flowed through her veins. "I love you, too, Reese. And you've mended both my heart and my soul."

"I don't deserve you," he muttered, but then he captured her mouth in a deep kiss.

She clung to his shoulders, enjoying every moment of his embrace. Finally, he lifted his head, allowing them both to capture their breath.

"Don't you think we deserve each other?" she teased.

"Maybe. But first there's something you need to know."

The seriousness of his tone made warning bells clang in the back of her mind. "Okay," she agreed. "What do I need to know?"

Reese took a deep breath, which only made her more nervous. "I won't ask you to marry me until I'm free of debt."

She was relieved it wasn't something worse, but still, how long would it take him to do that? "Reese, I don't care about money," she began.

"Don't," he interrupted. "The debt is mine, and I refuse to ask you to share it. This isn't negotiable, Katy. I couldn't stay away from you because I love you. I know I don't have a right to ask you to wait for me, but in the end, I decided that was your decision to make, not mine."

Her heart ached for him, but she understood where he was coming from. She didn't like it, thought it was ridiculous, but she couldn't help admiring him.

"I'm determined to start fresh with you," he said when she didn't answer. "So it's up to you where we go from here."

She smiled and stood up on her tiptoes to kiss him again. "I love you, Reese Webster," she whispered. "You are definitely a man worth waiting for."

"Thank God," he murmured.

Woof! Woof!

Katy giggled and glanced down at Duke, who was sitting patiently near Reese's feet, staring up at them as if asking what was taking so long already.

"You, too, Duke," she said, reaching down to stroke his silky fur. "You and Reese are a package deal."

Duke thumped his tail against the floor, obviously in full agreement.

EPILOGUE

Reese patted the ring reassuringly in his pocket as he strode up to Katy's front door. The last year had been good to him. His boss had given him a raise, and he'd trained two German shepherds for a nice profit. He'd doubled up his payments and had paid off the last of his outstanding bills three months ago.

He'd saved every dime since then for Katy's engagement ring. It was modest, but if she wanted something bigger, he'd oblige. The downside was that he'd be forced to push off any chance of a wedding for another couple months.

Her decision, not his. He'd do whatever she wanted, even if it killed him.

Which it just might.

He knocked at her door and nearly swallowed his tongue when he saw her standing there in an emerald-green figure-hugging dress.

"You look beautiful," he said in a husky tone.

"You look pretty good, yourself," she countered, noticing he'd dressed in the only nice clothes he owned, a pair of black dress slacks and a gray button-down shirt. "I know you said you made reservations, but I decided to cook for us instead."

"Katy, I wanted tonight to be special for you," he protested. As much as he loved her deep red hair, she could be awfully stubborn when she got an idea in her head.

"Trust me, having you over, cooking dinner for you, is special." Her smile faltered a bit. "Are you angry?"

He drew her in for a deep kiss. "Of course I'm not angry," he said when they could breathe. "Thank you for doing this."

She took his hand and led him into the living room, where she had candles lit and fresh flowers on the table. "I hope you don't mind, but I wanted to celebrate."

He thought of the ring he had burning a hole in his pocket. "It is a special day, isn't it? One year ago today, we acknowledged our love for each other."

Her eyes lit up. "You remembered!"

"Of course I remembered." Since the timing seemed right, he dropped to one knee, pulled out the ring and opened the case. "Katy Reichert, will you marry me?"

"Yes! Oh, yes! Of course I'll marry you!" She tugged him up off the floor and threw herself into his arms. It took him a minute to realize she hadn't even looked at the ring. "I love you so much," she murmured.

"I love you, too." He kissed her again and then pulled back so that he could slide the diamond ring on her finger. "If you don't like it, you can pick out something else."

"I love it," she assured him. "But I love you more."

"Good, I hope you don't mind a short engagement. Because I'm pretty much sick of waiting to make you my wife."

She laughed. "I love short engagements. And I'm sure Pastor John will fit us into his schedule as soon as possible."

"I love you, Katy," Reese repeated. "You've made me whole."

"We healed each other," she pointed out. "Now sit down or dinner will be ruined."

He did as she requested but knew that no matter what she served, dinner would be perfect.

Because they were together, at last.

If you enjoyed this book, please check out the first chapter of Christmas Reunion, a novella.

C hapter One

HOPE COUNTY SHERIFF'S Deputy Ian Kramer gripped the steering wheel tightly as he maneuvered the treacherous highway through the swirling snow. The citizens of Crystal Lake, Wisconsin were likely thrilled to have a white Christmas, but he was the one stuck working night shift over the holiday and patrolling the county in the middle of a blizzard was not his idea of fun.

Not that he was complaining. After everything that had happened with his brother a few months ago, he was lucky to have his job at all. He was very grateful that after a lengthy month-long investigation, Sheriff Luke Torretti had allowed him to return to duty. The graveyard shift wasn't his favorite, but he was willing to take whatever his boss gave him.

No way was he going to ruin the second chance he'd been given.

The wind kicked up, blowing snow horizontally across the country highway, buffeting his SUV. He was moving at a crawl and, thankfully, didn't see any traffic on the road. He hoped the townsfolk were smart enough to stay home rather than risking their lives driving through this.

No such luck. He carefully navigated a hairpin turn in the road, and caught a glimpse of dim flashers blinking on and off. As he approached he could see that a car was nose down, stuck in the ditch. The vehicle was covered in snow, so much that in another hour, even the flashers would be difficult to see.

If the battery held out for that long.

Ian slowed to a stop and peered through the windshield, trying to read the license plate so he could run the tag through the system. Unfortunately, the information was obliterated with snow. He contacted the dispatcher to let her know that he was responding to a stranded vehicle off Highway ZZ.

Warily, he slid out from the driver's seat, ducking his head and tugging his hat further on his head against the ferocious wind. He approached the driver's side door, but the foggy window made it impossible to see who was inside.

He sharply rapped on the window. "I'm Deputy Kramer," he shouted. "Is everyone all right in there?"

There was a long pause, and he doubted his voice carried above the howling wind. He tapped on the window again and to his surprise, it lowered, revealing the pale face of a woman.

"Kramer? Ian Kramer?" she echoed in surprise.

He bent over to get a better look, and his eyebrows shot up in surprise when he recognized the woman's heart-shaped face framed with long dark hair.

"Sarah Miller," he said in a shocked tone.

Her slight smile faded. "My last name is Franklin now. And that's my five-year-old son, Ben, in the backseat."

Sarah was married. And had a son. The news shouldn't have surprised him. After all, they'd only spent one summer together and that had been ten years ago. But the three months they'd shared together were forever etched in his memory. He'd fallen for Sarah hard, and ridiculously thought she felt the same way. Yet when summer had ended Sarah hadn't returned his phone calls. After a few weeks, he'd given up since he was attending college in Madison.

He'd never heard from her again.

Disturbing to realize that he'd never forgotten her.

"Hi, Ben," he said to the youngster curled up in a sleeping bag in the backseat. Where on earth was Sarah's husband? She shouldn't have been driving in this storm all by herself.

"I tried to call for a tow truck, but couldn't get through." Sarah shrugged. "I left a message with Billy's Auto Repair."

"Hank owns the garage, but unfortunately he's out of town," Ian said. "He's visiting his daughter in Madison and won't be back until after Christmas."

The spark of hope in her eyes dimmed. "I don't suppose you can somehow pull me out of the ditch?" she hesitantly asked.

He could, but there was no telling what damage had been done to her car, and he doubted that it was drivable. Besides, he'd rather get Sarah and her son somewhere safely out of the storm. "I'll give you a ride, and we'll work on getting your car unstuck later. Do you have a reservation at the hotel?"

"No. I'm heading to my grandparent's cabin. I appreciate you giving us a ride. Would you mind getting our suitcases out of the trunk?"

Suitcases? Ian thought it was odd that she'd come up to her grandparent's place two days before Christmas, but then again, for all he knew, her husband might be meeting her there so they could spend a rustic holiday together.

The idea left a sour taste in his mouth.

"No, I don't mind." He tried not to remember the last time he'd been to her grandparent's cabin, the night he kissed her beneath the stars. Ancient history, he reminded himself as Sarah popped the trunk.

There were three suitcases and several boxes crammed in the trunk without any room to spare. He couldn't help wondering just how long Sarah and her son were planning to stay. There was way more stuff here than what they'd need if they were just visiting over the holiday break from school.

Not that Sarah's plans were any of his business. He fought against the wind and swirling snow, grabbing the suitcases and hauling them over to store them in the back of his SUV.

Sarah joined him, looking cute in her pink parka with matching hat and gloves. "Ian, would you be willing to take the boxes too, if there's enough room?"

"Sure." He saw her son standing beside her, the hood of his coat up over his head and a scarf covering a good portion of his face. "Why don't you and Ben get inside where it's warm? I'll take care of moving everything over."

She nodded, looking relieved. "Thank you."

He trudged through the snow, until he had everything from Sarah's car—including the sleeping bag and booster seat from the backseat. Sarah wrestled with securing the booster seat while Ian kicked the snow from his boots and slid behind the wheel.

"Ready?" he asked as he started the engine and blasted the heat on high.

"Yes," Sarah's voice was strong as she glanced back at Ben, as if to reassure her son. "We're ready, right Ben?"

The boy paused, then nodded. "Right, Mom."

Ian nodded and slowly pulled back out onto the highway. He noticed that Ben hadn't said much, and his instincts warned him that something wasn't quite right with this situation.

He was surprised at how much he wanted to help and protect Sarah from whatever was causing the shadows in her eyes. But unless she was involved in something illegal, which he highly doubted, he needed to remember her problems weren't his concern.

He had his brother to worry about, and that was a huge challenge. Jesse was finally getting the psychiatric help he needed, but Ian was still worried about his brother's emotional stability. The last thing Ian needed was to put his job at risk, especially not for a married woman. He'd get Sarah and her son safely to her grandparent's cabin.

From there, she could call her husband for help if needed.

SARAH MOMENTARILY CLOSED her eyes and silently prayed, seeking strength. She'd never in her wildest dreams imagined that Ian Kramer was still living in Crystal Lake. Or that he was a deputy with the sheriff's department.

She'd been seventeen to Ian's eighteen during that summer they'd spent together. They'd been inseparable; swimming and boating in the lake, taking long walks on the hiking trail, and sitting by the campfire roasting marshmallows at night.

Ian had kissed her several times, nothing too heavy until the night before she had to leave to return home. They'd kissed beneath the stars, passion simmering between them. She was ashamed to admit that Ian had been the one to break things off before their young love spiraled out of control.

"Sarah? Are you all right?" Ian asked, breaking the silence.

She opened her eyes and took a deep breath, forcing a smile. "I'm fine, thanks so much for coming to our rescue."

"I'm surprised you decided to drive up here, despite the

storm warnings that have been on the news for the past twenty-four hours," Ian admitted.

She hoped the darkness hid the desperation she knew was reflected in her eyes. The minute she heard David, her ex-husband, was going to be released from jail, she'd loaded up her car and driven north. She hadn't heard the weather reports until she was on the highway, but even then she wouldn't have let the snow stop her.

"I was already on the road when I heard the news," she said, trying to keep her voice steady.

"I didn't realize your grandparents had kept the cabin," Ian said, shooting her a side long glance. "I thought maybe your family had sold it."

Sarah knew what he was really asking, since she hadn't returned his many phone calls ten years ago. And at the very least, she owed him an explanation.

"A week after returning home after our summer together, my mother was diagnosed with stage four uterine cancer. My father," she hesitated, unwilling to speak ill of the dead. "He didn't handle it well. Instead of being supportive he worked longer and longer hours, using every excuse possible to avoid coming home. Six months after my mother passed away, he died of a massive heart attack."

"Oh, Sarah, I'm sorry for your loss," Ian said, reaching out to take her hand. The simple comforting gesture made tears spring to her eyes and she struggled to blink them back before Ian noticed. "I can't imagine what you went through. Losing both your parents so close together must have been terrible. You should have called me, I would have been there for you."

Looking back, it was easy to see how different her life might have been if she'd garnered the courage to make that call. But then again, she wouldn't have Ben, and she could never regret having her son. Ben meant everything to her.

"I was pretty focused on staying in high school so I could graduate, and being there for my mother," she said softly. "And then so much time had passed, it didn't seem right to call you."

"I would have come, no matter when you called," he said, giving her hand a gentle squeeze before releasing her. She missed his warmth and twisted her fingers together to prevent herself from reaching for him.

Sarah knew she couldn't afford to let her foolish teenage emotions get the better of her. Ian had been the center of her world that summer, but the reality of her mother's cancer and her father's avoidance had caused her to push the memories aside. She'd convinced herself that he'd moved on without her.

And she'd moved on as well. Realizing too late that she'd made the wrong choice in marrying David.

But there was nothing to be gained by rehashing the past.

"Well, anyway, that's enough about my life. What about you?" she asked, eager to change the subject. "I'm so impressed that you're a sheriff's deputy."

He lifted a brow and sent her a sideways glance. "I'm pretty sure I told you that I wanted to be a cop when I grew up," he reminded her.

And she'd wanted to be a nurse. Regret burned in the back of her throat. She'd only managed to complete a nursing assistant program before her mother passed away.

"Yes, you did," she said softly. "I didn't start my nursing degree. I completed my nurse's aide training, but that's all." Which reminded her she'd need to get a job within the next few weeks, before she depleted her meager savings. But that would have to wait until after the holidays.

"We have a hospital here," he said, as if reading her mind. "Eighteen months ago, I spent more time there than I wanted to."

"What happened?"

He lifted a shoulder. "Gunshot wound, but I survived. The staff there took good care of me."

Sarah swallowed hard, more upset than she had a right to be about his close call. Why was she dredging up her old feelings for Ian? After ten years, they were two completely different people, nothing at all like the carefree teenagers they'd been.

"Are you married?" she asked, striving for a casual tone.

"Nope. Got close once, but things didn't work out."

Her own five year marriage proved that was the understatement of the year. Her divorce had been finalized over two years ago, but that hadn't stopped David from coming after her. And now that he'd been released from jail, her brief respite was over.

"Lucky that you found out ahead of time," she said before she could stop herself. "Less complicated that way."

Ian frowned. "Sarah, what's wrong? Why isn't your husband with you?"

She glanced over her shoulder, relieved to see that Ben had fallen asleep. "We're divorced," she said simply. "I haven't changed my name because of Ben. It's less complicated to share the same last name."

"I guess I can understand that," Ian said with a nod. "How long have you been divorced?"

"Two years." She had no idea why she was telling him this. It wasn't as if she was interested in picking up where their summer romance left off. The last thing she wanted was to jump into another relationship. Once was more than enough. "Oh, is that the driveway to my grandparent's place?" she asked, changing the subject as the highway marker caught her attention.

"That's it, although it might be tricky getting into the driveway," he cautioned. "Having four-wheel drive isn't fail-safe."

She refused to let the news upset her. She was more than willing to walk up to the cabin if necessary.

Ian gunned the engine and barreled through the snow drifts without stopping until he reached the clearing in front of the cabin. The welcome sight of the familiar rustic dwelling gave her an overwhelming sense of relief.

"Ben, we're here," she said, reaching back to shake her son awake."

He opened his eyes but then groggily closed them again.

"Let him sleep," Ian suggested. "I'll carry him in for you."

"I can do it," she said quickly. "But would you be willing to light a fire for us?"

"Of course. Do you have the key?"

She smiled. "Don't you remember? It's in the flower pot on the porch."

Ian looked surprised, but nodded. "I do remember. Stay here, let me check things out first."

"All right." She sat back in her seat, knowing she shouldn't be leaning on Ian like this. Hadn't she learned the hard way that it was better to stand on her own two feet? She'd vowed never to be dependent on a man again.

With renewed determination, she pushed her door open and tried not to gasp as she was hit by a blistering wave of cold air. Winters in Crystal Lake were far different than summers, that's for sure. Although they had tough winters in Chicago too. She refused to be wimpy.

After trudging around to the back of the police vehicle, she fumbled with the latch. After two tries she finally found the release. She grabbed the smaller of the suitcases and then closed the tailgate so the snow wouldn't get inside before heading up toward the cabin.

The door was open, which was a relief since that meant Ian had found the key. The interior of the cabin smelled musty and was only slightly warmer than being out in the wind and snow. The only light was from Ian's flashlight which was propped beside him.

"I told you I'd carry everything in," Ian chided gently from his kneeling position in front of the wooden stove.

"I know, but I'm not helpless, and I appreciate that you're getting the fire started." She glanced around the cabin, surprised to note that it didn't look all that much different from the last time she'd been here. Of course her grandparents had come up here on occasion over the years, at least until they'd retired in Arizona, but she hadn't been back.

Until now.

She walked into the small kitchenette and opened the drawers until she found a few candles and matches. She placed the candles around the room, the dancing flames helping to chase away the darkness.

When she walked over to the wood burning stove, she was pleased to see that Ian had gotten a small fire started from the wood that was stacked on the floor beside it. Maybe it was only her imagination, but it seemed like the interior of the cabin was already warming up from the fire.

Ian glanced up at her. "It will take me a while to get this going. Why don't you bring Ben inside? I'll get the rest of your stuff as soon as I'm finished."

She nodded. After all, Ben was her top priority. Before going back outside, she went into the smaller of the two bedrooms, grateful to see that the mattresses were still intact and hadn't been attacked by rodents.

They'd be fine using the sleeping bags for tonight, since she knew she'd have to sleep in the living room to keep the fire going anyway. Feeling certain they were safe here, she eagerly headed back outside to get her son.

After freeing him from the booster seat, she picked him up in her arms. Ben was large for his age, and she staggered a bit as she headed inside the cabin. Ian met her at the doorway and gently pried her son away, easily handling his weight.

"Hang on, I need to gab the sleeping bag." When she returned a few minutes later, her heart melted when she saw that Ian was holding Ben on his lap in front of the fire.

"We're at the cabin?" Ben asked, rubbing his eyes.

"Yes, we're here. You're going to use your sleeping bag tonight. Won't that be fun?"

Her son nodded and yawned. Ian stood and carried Ben into the bedroom, waiting for her to arrange the sleeping bag before lowering her son to the mattress.

She sat beside him, making sure he was tucked in.

"Mom? Dad's not going to find us, is he?" Ben asked.

Her heart clenched in her chest and tears pricked at her eyes as she leaned down to press a reassuring kiss on his forehead. "No, he's not going to find us. Go to sleep, okay?"

"Okay. Good night." Her son closed his eyes and curled up onto his side.

When she straightened, she found Ian's intense gaze boring into hers and knew with a sinking feeling that he wasn't going to leave until he knew the truth.

DEAR READER

I hope you're enjoying my Crystal Lake Series. I love adding pets into my stories and Duke is a German shepherd owned by a friend of mine, but her Duke isn't a trained police dog the way he is in this story.

There are six books in my Crystal Lake Series and I hope you check out each one.

Thanks to those of you who've written such wonderful reviews of my previous stories, Healing Her Heart and A Soldier's Promise and Coming Home. These reviews are very important and often help other readers discover great stories. I also love hearing from my readers and can be reached through my website at www.laurascottbooks.com. You can also sign up to receive my newsletters through my website, I only send them out to announce new releases and I do offer a free exclusive Crystal Lake Novella to all subscribers!

Yours in Faith,
Laura Scott